Songs of the Maniacs

Mickey J. Corrigan

ISBN: 0-9828482-9-3
ISBN-13: 978-0-9828482-9-6

Other Books by
MICKEY J. CORRIGAN:

The Ghostwriters

Ex-Treme Measures

The Blow Off

Sugar Babies

The Hard Stuff Series

Praise for Mickey J. Corrigan

"Mickey J. Corrigan spices up the same old short romance with a fun pulp fiction twist...quite possibly the best short e-book I've read in years."   *~Nights and Weekends*

"Mickey is one of my favourite authors and I can't wait to read more of her books."   *~Geeky Girl Reviews*

"This story reminds me of something you would see on the *The Twilight Zone*...If you are looking for something totally different in a love story, this is the book for you."
    ~Love Romance Passion

"Mickey J. tells it like it is, no frills, no flounces, just in your face. And that writing voice? Unbe-freaking-lievable. The woman is a born storyteller. That's an Irish trait, mind. And I knew she had Irish blood in her the minute I started reading her. I just knew it...The one thing which strikes me about this author is that she has a woman's voice – but she writes like a man."   *~Contemporary Romance Review*

"It's official. I am in love with Mickey J. Corrigan. Her writing style is all her own and I cannot get enough of it...There is no sugarcoating in a MJC book. Life is tough, but life is still good."   *~For the Love of Books and Alcohol*

Thanks to Jen and everyone at Salt Publishing; Jade and Regina at Lewd Pony Press; Mel and JP at home.

1.

A Moment

Victor and I are sort of friends, then we are sort of lovers, and later he has his hands around my throat. It is that kind of relationship.

He is choking me and I am coughing and he is saying, "If you want to escape from all of this, you have to work with me here." I start to see a blackness like an ink spot seeping into my vision from the corners of my eyes. "I know we can do this. Together," he is saying.

His voice is faint. And getting fainter. I gurgle and cough. Even this seems distant.

Something is lodged in my throat, something cold and hard. Victor's tight clasp on my neck is forcing the thing in my throat to edge up my windpipe or my esophagus or whatever.

I am choking and, at the same time, the blockage in my throat is coming loose.

Far away, a woman coughs. I guess this is me.

Victor continues to squeeze my neck. Drool from his contorted mouth drips and splashes on my cheeks. The spittle is cool. This turn in our relationship is an unexpected one. But so was sleeping together.

I could get fired for this. If I live.

I am staring up at the ceiling out of the middle of my eyes. Around the edges, the ink spot is spreading. Are those real stars I am seeing? Of course not. Those are stains, a splatter of stains on the ceiling that have seeped down from the floor above. Where have I seen that pattern before?

My memory is not what it once was.

But I can remember everything that happened today. Every detail. The way the day began with a morning in my office like any other, warm and well lit and lightly salted. Celia and her dreams. Justin and his photo. How the breeze turned cold and raw, ripping the palm fronds from their trunks and pitching rain against the window glass. The storm, Victor's cotton bathrobe, the quiet. The brown pelicans above the hard-packed beach sand. The toss of blue-green waves. Sasha. Ben. The noise and the smoke of the bar. Francis and the gun and the lawn man. The stink of cheese fries and that suffocating smell of gasoline.

The thing in my throat.

"When your dreams are more real than your reality?" Victor is speaking in a distant whisper. The air feels suddenly ice cold and the black folds in on itself and becomes even blacker. "Then which one is your real consciousness?"

Victor is talking in riddles, but I know what he's getting at.

The snake patch on a leather jacket.

The number one hundred and eleven.

A mirror with someone else's reflection.

A certain kind of personality. Smart, not slick.

When you really don't care about anything.

Interchangeable living beings.

SIPD, that is, Stand-in Personality Disorder, the epidemic transforming our world.

I am limp in Victor's hard grasp. My head sags forward. His hands have loosened their steely grip, but it is too late. It looks like this is it.

But wait. Are these the kinds of thoughts you have when you are dying? Most of these thoughts are fragmented. Random. And heavy with undisclosed meaning. Someone else's meaning.

How disappointing.

Here I am, limp and blue, dead in the arms of a violent lover, and all that flashes before my eyes are little pieces from *other* people's lives?

This is just so *me*.

"The self you believe is yourself is not the real you," Victor is saying. His voice comes to me in its smallest version, the one you hear from the far end of a long dark tunnel. I am thinking about the words floating on his gentle tongue and easing past his fleshy lips. Too bad he stopped kissing me and put his hands around my throat instead. Too bad he had to ruin the moment like this.

It always ends up badly with me and men.

"If we can destroy the false self, that will be our salvation. Yours and mine," comes Victor's voice from a pinpoint of light in an infinite black void.

From the vanishing point.

From the God upstairs.

I guess I made a sort of final decision today. Not entirely by choice, though. Decisions can be made through lack of choice. And some days can decide everything for you. Some days can choose you.

Today was that kind of day.

Or maybe I just fucked up.

2.

Let's rewind the memory reel and start from the beginning.

This is how the day begins. How it always begins for me.

The breeze is sweet and mild with only a pinch of salt. I can't smell the ocean, but I don't feel the tension of The City, either. My office window overlooks the quad and I am casually scanning the sidewalk for my ten o'clock. Celia may or may not show up this morning. Her lack of self-interest is her biggest problem and the main reason, in my opinion, she is not making any progress.

Most of the people here at this institution are like Celia.

That's the first thing you notice about the people here, the residents. They lack self-interest, yet they are completely self-involved. There seems to be a missing need to be loved. By self and others. It takes a while before you realize just what is strange about everybody here, but when you are trained to look for this trait, you can spot it within a few minutes.

I am trained to look for these kinds of traits. I am trained to diagnose subtle (and not so subtle) symptoms.

These people, the residents here, the ones who come to me, they are more and less themselves. They are no longer exactly themselves. First they are less. This may last for days, weeks or years. Then later on, quite suddenly, they are more. Much more.

I spend most of my time here, both my work time and my "free" time. (Really, what kind of time is *free?*) However, I am not a resident. Residents are the people with symptoms. I am not a dorm advisor either. Dorm advisors are the people without symptoms and, in my opinion, without heart. No, I am a translator. A listener. An expert ear tuned to the strange frequencies of others. To the pulsating songs of the troubled. To the troubling stories of the troubled residents and, sometimes, their families. And there are students who speak to me, too, men and women only a few years younger than myself.

They come from the nearby university and they are training to do the kind of work I do.

Some of the students are troubled too. After all, like seeks like.

This is not easy work. It requires technical skill, and a special type of personality. Almost a lack of personality, but one founded on a strong ego.

Personality is a kind of faith in one's inner meaning despite the absence of evidence to support this.

I did not choose my work, my work chose me. I have always been one of those women to whom others come to spill their guts, seeking not approval but solace and advice. Advice they almost always ignore. My personality, which I see as open and nonthreatening, fits their need for nonjudgmental guidance and support. I can listen to the most perverse fantasies and desires, the most disturbed dreams and ideas, the ugliest life details, without flinching or frowning.

Whatever.

It is exactly this type of uncritical response the people who confide in me are seeking.

The key is to care to help but not care who or what you are helping. To assist those in need while not acknowledging their needs.

To offer them total indifferent acceptance.

The air is still today, warm and still. I could be sitting in a greenhouse, the air is that wet and quiet, everything natural so beautifully tamed. The grass in the quad is a flat emerald carpet, recently mowed to perfection. Sleek palm fronds glisten and pose like on a postcard from paradise. Even the sun sits itself down on the wooden slats of the park benches below me in a benign shine.

The day is not what is seems, however. The local news channel is all excited chatter, experts full of dire warnings about another tropical wave in the Caribbean. Outside, the air is calm. The trees that outline the quad and spread back to cover the grounds, all this greenery stands silently. And the cloudless blue sky remains nonchalant.

This part of the world reminds me of a feral cat. Crouching here in the lap of the sun, lounging and lazing, but full of a secret primal urge to pounce. See all those palm fronds waiting to leap out, to clutch and choke? Everything becomes a weapon in certain situations.

I catch a glimpse of the thinning orange crown of Celia's head as she slips in the front door of the building, which is directly under my office window. Surprise,

surprise. Maybe she has something to say to me today. Maybe an insight has come to her. One never knows with the residents here.

What I do here mostly is what I call "ears and verbiage." I listen carefully and at length, then I offer my professional and personal opinions in the form of words. The kind of words that dissolve in the air like sugar on a wet tongue. Disposable words. Soft, pliant words that have only a temporary effect. Nothing lasts around here, not with these people. That's the second thing you notice about them. Their complete lack of continuity.

There is a demanding, childlike knock on the door, which is half open, and Celia slides into my office. She is a small woman with a knobby face and overly flexible extremities that make her appear spring-loaded. If she had any energy left she might be bouncy, but Celia drags her bones to the long butterscotch sofa against the far wall and collapses. In a heap.

The brass and glass clock on the wall above the sofa clicks in a brittle way each time the second hand sweeps past the twelve. I should get a new clock, a quiet clock, but I've been forgetful lately. I spend too much time thinking about the people here. The residents and their battered, worn out personalities. Their wasted lives, their once rich buttercream lives, reduced now to dry crumbs.

Everyone here once had a deep-dish dessert of a life compared to the ones they are living now. Now everyone settles for leftovers, or goes without.

Celia wears a sea green hospital gown and a matching plastic bracelet. On the bracelet her name and dorm are typed in tiny black letters. She is not required to dress like a hospital patient, but for Celia, life has come to this. Dressing like a mental patient is a style that suits her outlook.

Her hospital pants are gathered at the waist with a drawstring, but she has to hold them up because she is so thin. Skeletal. Talk about thigh gap. I remember when I first met Celia, she had a trim but fit body, the kind of body a young woman takes to the gym four or five days a week and runs on the treadmill for at least forty-five minutes.

We have a gym here but exercise is suggested, not mandatory. Mostly the dorm advisors use the gym. Late at night, it is rumored, some of these men (big men, they are all big men) lift weights and smoke weed when they are supposed to be watching over the residents. There's an Olympic-size outdoor pool here too, where the residents can swim on especially hot days. Some of them just sink into the popsicle blue water and wait there until one of the dorm advisors pulls them out.

Celia lifts her head for a moment and looks at me, then slumps again. She might have taken a little too much Adjuster this morning. Adjuster is the current mental straitjacket of choice. When the residents lie around a lot, it can be from too much of this month's flavor of pharmaceutical. Sometimes it's from the condition itself, though, from the damaged personality. It's hard to tell.

I clear my throat and that seems to perk her up.

"I feel like I'm still in last night's dream," she mumbles. "Do you ever feel like you can't get out of your dreams?" I smile encouragement, so she continues. "I guess I'm starting to realize I'm awake. It just feels wrong somehow, though, you know?"

I ask her if she would like a glass of water, and she says no. Then she looks at me carefully. "I guess I can tell you the dream. No harm in that. You already know how nuts I am." What passes for a smile flickers across Celia's craggy and crinkled features. Her flesh has shrunk but not her skin, so it hangs oddly from her bones. Like those clear plastic bags they put around your dry-cleaning. "You know how it is," she says.

The clock clicks over. Water beads and slides on my plastic bottle of Diet-Water.

"This time I was a man," Celia starts in, sitting up a little straighter on the couch. "This time I was a man who liked to hurt women."

All the residents tell stories like this.

Dreams are stories. Stories you tell yourself when you are asleep. And your life? Your life is a story too. Your life is the story you tell yourself about yourself. When you are awake.

And the truth is, every story has an unhappy ending. This is a truth you have to accept. If you cannot accept this truth, you might end up in a place like this. Trying to rewrite your story. Over and over.

As Celia tells me her unhappy dream, the unhappy story inside her head, the unhappy truth of her life, I say nothing. I do nothing. I simply listen, my face a blank sheet of paper for her to write her words on, a flat mirror she can look in and see a reflection of herself. A self that does not look back in anger or distaste.

Celia goes on. And on. She unwinds her story, the tangle of images, her dream of childhood torture and abuse. Tears run down her crumpled bag of a face.

"What does it mean?" she asks me. "Why do I dream I'm these horrible men all the time? In my dreams now *I'm* the people I've always been most afraid of. Why? Why can't I just have normal dreams?"

I hand her the Kleenex box and Celia wipes her bleary eyes. It is time for verbiage, so I indulge her. I tell her the dreams are part of her illness and it is good for her to air them, let them dissipate. I tell her everyone here has dreams like this, dreams in which we are terrible people who do terrible things. There is no escaping the dreams. We must accept them and try to be strong.

"Do *you* have ugly dreams?" Celia asks me, her head cocked, the damp tissue balled in her fist. Palm fronds rustle as the wind picks up slightly, a tease.

"Yes," I say. "I have awful dreams too."

Perhaps these kinds of dreams are, in fact, normal dreams. In this time and place, who can say? This is what I tell Celia and she smiles. I can see her once pretty face sunk deep in the crêpe paper skin drooping from her skull.

Before she came here, Celia had a life. College student, bank teller, partier with lots of lovers. "I don't remember my dreams from that time," Celia says. "I slept like a baby, though."

Now she sleeps in a dorm room with six single beds lined up along one pale green wall. Home to Celia is a numbered room on a long drab hall of identical rooms in a squat brick building specially designed for troubled women.

She sits back against the couch and stares at me from under heavy lids. Her eyes have no life in them. She is a shell. A crust.

"The guilt in these dreams is awful," she whispers. "But the sex is fucking fantastic. So what the hell does it mean?"

It means Celia is becoming more herself. Her condition is advancing, that is, she is deteriorating in the same manner all the residents do. It appears to be the natural course of the condition. This is what I regard as self-improvement through total self-destruction.

I cock my head, noncommittal. "You tell me," I encourage. "What do you think it might mean?"

"I don't know," Celia says, hesitating. She inhales so deeply her nostrils flare. "But I will say this: I'm scared. Because this morning?" She hesitates and looks down at her lap, where she is picking at the plastic hospital bracelet with her ragged, chewed-up fingernails. "This morning, right before I came over? When I looked in the mirror over the bathroom sink, I almost fainted. Because *there was nothing there.* Where *I* should have been, I mean. Instead, I was looking straight into the eyes of a stranger. A man. A big, ugly, awful man. I froze, then as quick as I could I turned around. *There was nothing there.* Nothing. No man. I turned back to the mirror. And there *he* was. Instead of me."

First you become less yourself. Then you become more yourself. Much more.

But I do not say this to Celia. No, I hand her the disposable words she has come for. My words of comfort and reassurance melt in the air between us. Celia's hollow eyes drift off as if she is already thinking about other things.

Outside, the wind whistles as it cuts across the quad and speeds west toward the far side of the world.

3.

When I was a child I went unscathed. My life was simple and free. At least in my child mind it appeared this way. I had two loving parents, we lived in a comfortable house in the Miami suburbs, and my three older brothers adored me.

Two of my brothers are residents here. They both have been institutionalized for quite a few years. In fact, they came here soon after SIPD was officially identified by the American Psychological Association as a new (and rampant) personality disorder. SIPD was not yet epidemic, more a curiosity than a disaster. Once I took on my position here, I was able to arrange a semiprivate room for my brothers, and we receive a family discount which cuts the tuition down to a manageable fee.

My other brother has been missing for more than a year. When I visit with Thom and Kip, we all speculate on Franny's life of mystery. Both of them think he split because he couldn't face coming here to visit, seeing his siblings deteriorate. I disagree. Franny is the oldest and the most responsible. So he is also the most screwed up. In my opinion, Franny needed to separate from us in order to become who he is. Rather than remain who we want him to be. More or less.

But this is the way I look at everyone. It is my training to seek such motivations in people. Especially in people who appear to have lost all motivation.

Celia has left behind the sour scent of disinfected wounds. I write a few clinical notes in longhand on a legal pad while I sip my Diet-Water. I should go grab some lunch at the café across the quad but I don't feel like rushing. Instead I finish my drink, which tastes more like nothing than nothing itself, and I stare out the window at the wind. There is nothing to see, but you can look for what would be there if the wind could make more of itself.

A hurricane is a good way to see the wind reaching for its potential.

The sparse ficus trees flutter a bit. The curly brown leaves that have blown off their branches whisk across the sidewalks with each stray gust. Fat bushes sporting yellow, peach, and red hibiscus blooms blot up the sharp noontime light. The flowers cling tightly to their thin stems whenever the breeze picks up.

I watch as a pair of three-foot long iguanas mate quickly on a shady scatter of leaves under an overgrown sea grape tree. A hundred feet away, a couple of neon orange males bob their heads at one another, vying for territory or some female hidden from view in the trees. People walking through the quad are stepping around the iguanas, allowing a respectful berth. This is mating season and the males tend to act aggressively when breeding.

What makes us think we are so different from the animals?

The clock ticks over and I look up. Lately, the time has seemed to flow more rapidly, as if headed downstream.

Franny would tell me I'm finally grown up and that's why time seems different to me now. I can picture him saying this to me, a wet laugh at the back of his long pale throat. When I imagine him sitting here on the couch in his black leather jacket with the snake patch on the shoulder, he has a smirk on his handsome face. He always used to smirk and say to us, "Guys: Be smart, not slick."

Sometimes when I imagine Franny sitting here across from me, he is staring down at his hands, his jacket creaking whenever he shifts position. Sometimes he looks up at me and there are two dark basins full of stagnant and unmoving water where his hazel eyes should be. Nothing stirs, and then he is gone.

"Knock, knock. Anybody home?"

Victor is a symptomless resident whose presence here baffles me. He likes to drop by and chat when I am between visitors. I am no closer to understanding him after months of daily banter. He exhibits a wholesome amount of self-interest, enough so that he exudes a kind of angry-guy sexual energy that I find annoying and arousing.

I wave him in and Victor plops down on the couch as always. He wears a worn pair of cutoff jeans, a white tank-top, and a day or two of beard. I can smell his athletic sweat. He's come from the gym or a jog around the grounds. Victor never reeks of fear and self-loathing like the other residents. This makes him strange, untrustworthy.

"Why do you drink that stuff?" he asks, pointing to my empty bottle of Diet-Water. "You're already too thin. A woman like you should savor the flavors of life. To serve as a role model," he adds quickly.

Victor tries to goad me out of my professional demeanor. He's good at it. Too good at it.

When I ask him why he is here today, which is what I ask him every time he comes by, Victor smiles. His big front teeth overlap slightly in an adorably boyish way. He stretches out his muscular legs and crosses them at the ankles. His basketball shoes are dirty and scuffed.

"I'm here for the company," Victor says. Then he looks at my breasts, grins, and nods his head. Victor is twenty-seven going on seventeen. I squirm in my seat. "When are you going to admit that you want me here? You want me as much as you've ever wanted any man," he says, then laughs.

We go through the I'm-going-to-have-to-ask-you-to-leave routine for a minute before I relax. I'm trying to remain professionally distant, but he's making it difficult.

"If you let me stay I'll tell you a dream I had. A dream I had before I came here," Victor says instead of getting up to leave.

I sit back in my chair, cross my arms over my breasts, and listen.

"I've had this dream five or six times. Always the same dream, with minor but essential variations. Like a really good song played by really different bands."

He pauses and strokes his overgrown sideburns where they meet his incoming beard. Dirty shoes, failure to shave, dreams that repeat themselves and lend themselves to discussion. Victor may not be symptomless after all. I tell him to tell me all about it.

I give good ear.

"The dream goes like this. I'm driving into The City to see a girl. I'm behind the wheel of my '66 Mustang with the top down, so I'm not speeding. I'm in my lane, enjoying myself. There's really no reason to speed in a classic car. You want to let everybody see what you've got."

He pauses and looks at me. For what? Approval? Admiration? Envy? Men seem to want something extra from me every time. I stare back, my face an open window he can look out to see his own back yard. His own highway lines.

Whatever.

"The sunset is rosy with air pollution and the air is thick with car fumes, but it's a perfect tropical evening and I'm cruisin'. I'm listening to Kanye. Totally chill. Then I pop in an oldies CD and the wind is combing my hair for me like the long cool hands of a long cool woman in a black dress, and I'm singing along with the music and then..."

Victor shakes his head back and forth a few times, then looks at me. "That's how it ends. With nothing. It ends every time with nothing." Victor gives me a rueful smile. "Now you tell me what that means to you. Then we can get going on things. Together."

I say nothing. The wind shrieks for a minute and we both glance out the window. Sunshine spills across the quad like shards of glass. We stare at one another.

"What's with the fucking iguanas, eh? Everywhere you go, big ugly reptiles. Grunting and humping one another."

Victor stands up and strides over to my desk. He leans across it to place a hand against my right cheek. His sweat smells fresh with a tinge of lime. Key lime. His smooth palm is warm and gentle on my skin.

"I'm tired of talking. Why don't we try to feel something, you and me? Us, baby. Why don't we try to feel something together?"

He strokes my face and I turn slightly so I can hold onto his fingers with my front teeth, softly. The fingers taste salty, like little minnows. I would guess his

29

body would taste like one big salt lick. I bite down. A metallic taste fills my mouth.

Victor pulls his hand away. "Jesus. The prisoner awakens."

It always comes to this with me and men.

"This place, you don't get it, do you?" Victor says as he lifts his wounded hand to his lips. Victor has nice pillowy lips. I could fall asleep on those lips. "Here's a hint. Think about stars. How the stars you see are dead but the light still comes here. Why is this true? Because we are all living in the past but we don't even know it."

Whatever.

I need to stop looking at Victor's lips. He is sucking on his hand, staring at me like he needs something I am unable to provide. So I stand up and point to the door.

I don't feel anything when he leaves. I'm a professional and I have a job here, and he's either a resident or an employee with serious problems. Does he know who he is? Does he know who I am?

No need to talk myself out of anything.

It's 12:30 and there is time yet before my next visitor. Later today, I will walk to the sea and back. I will enter the mouth of the wind and maybe I will get swallowed up in the storm.

Maybe then I will feel something more, rather than something less.

4.

When Justin sits down on the couch I turn from the window with a start. He is like a ghost, appearing without the sound of approaching footsteps, so thin he seems to shimmer. He brings a suck of cold air into the room with him.

He lies down, flat on his back, staring at the ceiling in the dead man's pose. I look at his emaciated body and think I will never be able to help Justin recover. But his symptoms will go away and he *will* leave here. He has Stage IV SIPD. So do many of my visitors.

Stand-in Personality Disorder is widely regarded as a treatable disease. According to all the latest scientific research and ongoing reports in the medical literature, that is. According to all the professionals and the institutions they run, the drug companies and the universities funded by them. All the blah blah blah says SIPD is a treatable disorder.

When looked at on an individual basis, however, *treatable* is the word. Because as a professional in the field, I have never known anyone to recover. People do have their symptoms disappear. They certainly do leave here and not return. But I have not seen anyone fully recover. Because the truth is, out of everyone here who has SIPD (and they all have SIPD in some stage or another), not one of them has been able to recover the self. And it is my opinion that when you fail to recover the self, then you fail to recover. Isn't that the definition of a cure, to recapture the whole self? Perhaps the post-postmodern self is too malleable for recovery. Maybe the psychic internal forces accompanying SIPD work to change the self irreparably.

I am having difficulty accepting this as a new kind of truth. But I am afraid that it is an unspoken truth for our time. And, when I am totally honest with myself, I will admit this difficult truth: I am not helping to cure anyone, not really.

Justin lies still, his yellowed eyes staring straight up. The ceiling, when I look, has wet spots. Something must be leaking in the office located on the floor above me. The water has created an expanding galaxy of stars above our heads.

Finally Justin turns to me and smiles. His teeth have fallen out and, even though he is around my age, he looks a hundred years old. He waves one bony arm at nothing, his pathetic panhandler smile fading. Then he begins to talk, and I let him.

"Most of the world's population dies within a few miles of where they were born. Most of the world's residents never go out into the world to see what the world has to offer them. Or take from them. And they are so afraid. They are afraid of losing the little they have. The trinkets, the old yellowed photographs, the crumpled newspaper articles about their puny accomplishments or the deaths of loved ones."

He wipes at the sticky spittle on his withered lips with the back of a hand cross-stitched with blue veins. Outside, the palm fronds slap one another. It sounds like someone shuffling a new deck of cards.

"Let me tell you what I know. I tell you this from a specific perspective, the perspective of the person who takes away. Because I am a thief. But I am a good thief. I relieve others of the useless material items that hold them from their futures. It is only when the overwhelming weight of their meaningless past is lifted that they are free

34

to explore life with a pure and unfettered heart. The way of the good thief is to quietly come into a life only to unchain it from its most beloved burdens."

Justin uses a bony finger (and that's all it is, a bone with a cellophane wrapping of flesh) to point to the ceiling. "If there's a God upstairs, he should do something about the rampant materialism that has destroyed us. Even the poorest parts of the world now, even the most remote edges of China and Africa and India. Even the South American jungles that once offered a harbor from the onslaught of consumerist culture, even the tiniest island in the middle of some unnamed sea. Everywhere you look there is too much product and not enough soul. If I had an army of thieves, I could never strip it all away."

He sighs heavily and closes his watery eyes. I know what he means. But that's our way of life, and one must accept life in order to live among the living.

Justin then recounts a primitive sexual fantasy in a dull monotone. There's too much food, booze, and me in Justin's fantasy life.

I doodle on my legal pad and say nothing. If he's looking for my disapproval, Justin does not find what he is looking for. My face remains impassive. My face is a portal, a hole through which he can see his history, his former life, the life he thinks he wants now.

Whatever.

Justin sits up and puts his standard issue paper slippers back on his bluish feet. He hums faintly, a melody that sounds like "Comfortably Numb." Then he smiles at me, baring his blackened dog's gums in a ghoulish attempt at good humor.

"You don't seem to care what I'm telling you here. Your face lacks affect. These things could be interpreted as symptoms." He raises his forehead where his eyebrows should be but are not. "Doesn't that worry you?"

He is taunting me. It always comes to this. Justin may be the walking dead, but he is still a man like all men. A man who feels powerless, yet somehow superior simply for being a man.

I tell him I believe his symptoms are abating. I tell him his fantasies are healthy ones. To want to eat, drink, and have sex, these are the fantasies of a healthy person.

Justin laughs as he stands to leave. His laugh sounds fifty years younger than he looks.

"If what I just told you is a 'fantasy,' then how do you explain this pretty little coed?" he asks. He walks toward my desk slowly, his hand outstretched. He drops a wadded piece of paper in front of me. Thick, yellowing paper. Photo paper. Old, damp, wrinkled up photo paper.

By the time I have unfolded the photo, Justin is at the door. He watches me to see the shock register on my face. "Aha!" he cries gleefully. "Affect is still possible. There's hope for you yet." He pauses, but I refuse to look up. "You seem like a smart girl, so why don't you think about this," he says. "All people are interchangeable. We each believe we are unique, yet as living beings we are as interchangeable as clouds in the sky."

I hear him shuffle away.

The photo in my hands is an original. The same one that appeared in my college yearbook. In the photo I am smiling and, honestly, I *am* a pretty little coed.

What is chilling is how I look. I look so sure of myself.

5.

A good bartender has to have a certain kind of personality. He or she must be friendly, open to all kinds of people and their intimate talk, and willing to listen to all sorts of crazy drunken stories.

I have that kind of personality.

To pay my way through college, I worked downtown at McGoren's Neighborhood Bar. I poured generous drinks and earned generous tips, especially from the male customers. I met my lovers at work. I rarely went to their homes or got to know their families, friends, and favorite dogs. A night with one of my lovers consisted of drinking and screwing in my rundown studio apartment.

Sound boring? It wasn't.

Some of my lovers didn't like my appetites, my limitations. Some of them never came into the bar again after a night of panting and slobbering all over my naked body. Some of the men I took home for beers and fancy finger work would continue to hang around the bar on the nights when I was on. Some of these men would drink together, and eventually they would end up talking to one another. I developed a reputation.

Perhaps I should say I *earned* a reputation.

I cannot tell you any of their names. I cannot recall a single one of their faces. My lovers from the neighborhood bar were interchangeable.

So I know exactly what Justin means. And I *am* a smart girl. So I will think about this more. I will think about how a shrunken head, a yellow creature with Saran Wrap for flesh, a walking dead man, could have come into possession of a photo of me. A portrait of me from that time, the time in my life when I listened to men talk at night under dim lights in rooms that smelled of cigarettes, whiskey, and nervous sweat. And sex. And me, these rooms smelled of me.

I will think about this. But not right now. Right now, I am walking across the quad to the café. I plan to buy a chicken salad plate and a large glass of Diet-Sweet iced tea. I plan to sit outside at a small round cement table

39

and enjoy what is left of the sunlight before the thick paste of grey cloud that is headed this way descends on us.

The wind has stiffened and the coconut palms bow toward me in the push of warm wet air. I have to veer off the sidewalk here and there to avoid the scattered iguanas sprawling about in the diminishing sunshine. It smells faintly of grapefruit blossoms and baked asphalt. I wish I felt hungry, but I do not.

I cannot remember the last time I ate anything that tasted memorable.

"If there is a God upstairs," Justin had said. But upstairs from where he had been sitting, upstairs from where he lay down on his bony back on the couch, there is only another room, another office of some sort. A room where something is leaking onto the floor.

This image bothers me. If all people are interchangeable, maybe all rooms are as well.

The café is empty and the glass doors to the cafeteria inside are locked. Aluminum shutters cover the outdoor counters. Administration must be concerned about the coming storm, so they've let all the employees go home. The vending machines are operational, of course, so I feed them dollar bills until they give me back a package of peanut butter crackers and a plastic bottle of

Diet-Sweet iced tea. The wind lifts my hair around my head and my skirt flies up in a sort of Marilyn Monroe arc.

The cement picnic bench is still warm but the clouds have closed in overhead. I like to watch the pretty blue sky disappear on days like this. I like to see the innocent blue get swallowed up in greedy bites by the mean blackness. I eat a few crackers and watch the advancing darkness begin to change the landscape before me. Everything is gradually altered from pleasant to eerie. The transformation only takes a few minutes.

All the iguanas scurry up the trunks of the sea grape trees to hide as the first few drops of rain splatter onto the sidewalk. I can smell the cool air rushing in to fill some type of vacuum. The wind whips the palm fronds back and forth like windshield wipers on the sky.

I should run back across the quad, but I don't. I feel like I am locked in a room, a glass room with no exit.

I stand up and move to shelter myself against the doors of the cafeteria. I am huddling under the café's perky red and white striped awning. My white blouse is soaked through in spots and sticking to my flesh. I won't be able to make it back to my office without looking like I've been in a wet T-shirt contest.

A man is coming across the quad wearing a bulky black raincoat and a yellow plastic hat. When he has the wind at his back he runs toward me. But then the wind shifts itself and he seems to pause and waver before pushing ahead once more. I fold my arms across my chest to cover myself, but the wind lifts my skirt again. The situation is hopeless. Dignity is not going to happen for me out here. I guess it has come to this.

The man comes closer, pushing and swimming through the heavy air, breast stroking his way against the western wind.

Breast stroking? Of course. It's Victor in the rain gear, Victor with an extra rain poncho in his hands and a big grin on his wet face. He can laugh all he wants to, I am grateful to him for rescuing me.

"Didn't your parents ever teach you to come in out of the rain?" he snickers as I slip the plastic coat over my head.

I grab his arm and we brace ourselves to head back across the quad. The clouds bear down on us and the wind smacks our bare faces with an icy rain. The air is at least ten degrees colder than when I came across the grass to the café. Behind us, the glass doors rattle loudly, shaking in their aluminum frames in the face of the gusting storm.

Looks like the tropical wave is here. I ask Victor what his plans are for the next few hours of wind and rain and nighttime skies. He puts his arm around me as we wade through the streaming puddles that suddenly swamp the low sides of the sidewalk. My pumps are ruined. My teeth are chattering.

"Maybe you ought to come up to my place and we can dry off. Together," he yells into my ear.

The wind screeches through the ficus hedges and under the eaves of my building. The street is empty except for rushing water with its catch of swirling leaves. Multicolored hibiscus blooms swirl across a river of rainwater.

When the street lamps switch on automatically in the premature darkness, we are at the front door. Victor opens it and I pass through. "I'm right upstairs from your office," he says with an odd smile. Before I am able to respond he reaches for my hand. "You never asked where I lived. All this time and you never asked."

6.

Anders mows the lawn at the big hotel for sick people. It's a good job. Anders is grateful for his job. He has been working at the big hotel since he was just twenty. That was a long time ago. Anders is not sure how long, but now he is older than that, older and more mature. And bigger.

Anders is a big eater. He likes his food, yes, he does. He likes cheese fries and cheeseburgers and cheesecake too. Anders eats at the cafeteria every day. He is allowed to eat only one serving, he can't come back up to the counter for more.

Where the hotel is, the weather is almost always warm. And the grounds are huge. He is responsible (yes, he has responsibilities) for trimming the ficus hedges and the brown branches on the palm trees. So, by the time he mows all the grass and then goes all around the hotel grounds trimming, it is almost time for Anders to start cutting the grass again.

Anders works weekends. But that's okay because he takes Wednesdays off. He hangs out with the dorm advisors whenever he can.

The dorm advisors like to hang out in the gym together. They live in The City like Anders does, but when they work the night shift they go to the gym and hang around. They let him listen while they sit by the ice machine, drinking can after can of beer and talking. Talking trash, the dorm advisors call it.

Anders likes to listen to that kind of trash. He likes to listen while the dorm advisors discuss the things in life he knows very little about. Like women. And what to do with them when everyone has their clothes off. And money, how to make more of it or lose it all. They talk about the doctors and the sick people. Who is hot and who is gonzo. How they are changing and what this looks like close up.

Anders cannot tell them apart, the sick people and the doctors. Only some of the sick people wear hospital pajamas, and only some of the doctors wear white hospital coats. So Anders can never be sure about most of the people he sees wandering around the hotel grounds.

But Anders likes to watch the sick people change. He is continuously amazed at how this happens. First they look like anybody staying at a hotel. Slowly they start to change, they grow thin and weak, like a person does who is sick. They look half dead! Anders gives up hope. But then (and this is the amazing part) they start to look healthy again. But different than when they arrived. Totally different.

Sometimes they become better looking, sometimes uglier. Sometimes they end up looking so bad it's scary. But they always end up different.

Anders doesn't understand how it works, but he would like to try it. He would like to change too. Not that he is sick. He isn't. Still, Anders would like to be one of the people who change.

Who would he change into if he could change? Anders has someone picked out. The perfect person to change into.

Anders would like to be a listener. In a skirt that blows up, up, up in the wind. He would like to become a woman who gets rescued in a storm when she is all wet and cold.

He hasn't figured out yet how he might do this, how he might change. He only wishes that this could happen to him one day. So far, he is still Anders. Big eating, hotel lawn mowing, slow thinking and never changing, Anders.

7.

His office is like mine in dimension and location above the quad, but there the similarities end. I stand stunned, glancing around what appears to be a cozy apartment. His places is so homey. A living space that feels well lived in.

I am dripping on his thick pile carpeting so I remove the loaner poncho, my sodden shoes and hose. I stare out the window at a familiar view. It is my view, but from a higher angle. Everything below looks a bit smaller and just a little farther away.

Suddenly the window looks out through a waterfall. The rain is heavier, torrential, splashing itself against the bricks of the building with a barrage of resounding slaps.

Victor returns to the living room and hands me a thick black towel, a plaid cotton bathrobe. He turns his back while I remove my blouse and skirt, which I drop on top of my other clothes on the carpet. The pile is growing. So is the puddle of water underneath the pile.

Victor turns back with a lewd grin. Then he strips off his rain gear and plops down on one of the two powder blue couches facing one another in the center of the room. He bends down to remove his basketball shoes. When he motions to the couch behind me, I back up to it, then sit. The upholstery is puffy and warm.

"While you and your clothes dry off, why don't I tell you what I'm doing here," Victor says.

My hair is dripping down the back of my neck, down the slope of my spine. And my clothes will stay wet if we leave the pile sitting in the center of the barfy green carpeting, where the rainwater has formed a shallow lake.

We stare at one another. Neither of us moves to pick up the clothes, to wring them out properly and hang them up to dry in the bathroom. I lean my wet head against the fat pillows of the powder blue couch.

"Go ahead," I say. "Try me."

Even without my clothes, or maybe especially without my clothes, I am the one with the upper hand here. I cross my legs and wriggle my chilly toes.

49

Predictably, Victor stares at my legs. The rain pelts the glass, the bricks, the tiles on the roof. Time passes this way. Time often passes this way.

"Do you look at a bagel and think how there is something lacking because there is a hole in the middle of it? Or do you wonder instead about the absence of dough that has made the bagel into what it is?" Victor pauses and we stare at one another. "I need to tell you about your dreams," he says.

I uncross my legs. *What about telling me what you're doing here, like you said? And without speaking in riddles,* I want to say. What I am thinking is, what am *I* doing here? But I say nothing.

"You dream about mowing the grass," he tells me. "You dream about an endless landscape of lush wild greenery that you must cut back and reduce and change endlessly. It is what you do. You are like the absence of dough. You are nothing, yet you are important. You have important work to do. You work to modify everything in order to meet the demands and expectations of an unknown God."

Victor gets up and goes into another room, a small kitchenette. Why doesn't my office have a cute little kitchen? He runs the water, opens and closes the cabinets.

Soon I can smell the rich brew, a dark roast coffee. Then he stands before me like a waiter in a fancy French restaurant. Two oversized mugs of steaming java sit on a mucous green plastic tray I recognize from the residents' dining hall. The mugs are from Big Boy Bagel Deli downtown, so there are pink cartoonish bagel faces on the white ceramic. In the place of a bagel hole, these hideous bagel faces each have a wide open mouth. Each bagel eats another bagel. Russian dolls in a fun house mirror.

I reach for a coffee mug and thank Victor.

"You think you are saying something but you aren't. You think I am seductive but I am not. You think you might help me by listening to me like you do with the others but this is an illusion."

Victor sits down across from me and rests the tray on his knees. Steam is rising from his lap. I have a slight urge to snicker.

"Your cognition is a dream, an elaborate hallucination," he states.

His voice is so ominous I want to jeer and roar with laughter. But I don't.

He sets the tray on the rug between us. Too much green, both the particular shade I think of as hospital green. It has always made me sad, that vomitous color.

The mirth slips away and I look beyond Victor to the wetness outside while I sip my coffee.

"Everyone changes places eventually," Victor says. "We all start out small and helpless. All around us are people with more power. Time goes by. At some point we find that we are in charge of our lives. Sometimes we have power over others. We do a good job, we fuck up. No matter what, eventually we are back where we started. Small and helpless once again."

Victor looks at me over the top of his coffee mug. "I'm going to tell you about myself," he says. "I need you to listen. *Only I can help you.*"

I don't laugh at him but I could. Sometimes the people who come to me are under the illusion they are there to help me. But Victor's apartment is something else. He lives like a dorm advisor in a building I believed was set aside for professional offices. I'm confused about this, and mildly upset. Why does he get two couches and a kitchenette? Is he a professional who lives here, or is he some sort of VIP resident? Who is this guy?

Victor stares into my eyes for a moment, then looks away. "You've got this all wrong. I really do want to help you. Can you try to listen to what I'm saying? I'd like to get through to you." He seems angry now, his voice too loud.

I draw my legs up into the lotus position and Victor sighs. Then he comes over to the couch and bends down to reach for me. I close my eyes and wait. A man like all men. Sometimes certain steps must be taken, specific things must be completed, before anyone is ready to listen.

After a minute, I open my eyes. Victor is kneeling before me. We look into one another's eyes. I can see my reflection in the glassy shine of his pupils. There I am, a tiny white flicker in the deep pools of an unknowable man. I feel something ticklish in the back of my throat.

Victor returns to the other couch, talks without looking at me. "I grew up in a small town north of Boston. My parents were school teachers in a small private boys' school and we lived in a nice apartment on campus. I was smart but not exceptional."

I sip my coffee and listen. I have heard it all before, different versions of the same story. Same story, different men telling it. Sometimes women. It does not matter in the long run, the story will have an unhappy ending. Maybe after he finishes talking he will tell me something I don't already know. It doesn't matter to me either way.

Whatever. At least the coffee is good.

"At UMass I majored in psychology because I liked medicine and people, but I knew I would never be able to afford medical school. I worked as a resident advisor in the dorms all the way through my Ph.D." Victor sweeps his right hand to indicate the apartment. "So I've lived in places like this all my life. This is home to me. That explains why I'm here. I understand this now. But it took me a while to realize where I was and why I was here. I can see you're struggling too. I want to help you out. Maybe together we can move beyond this."

I have no idea what Victor is talking about. But this doesn't surprise me. He has told me what I wanted to know. He is a resident. Due to his training in psychology, he must have received special permission to live here in the office building.

I nod encouragement. "Go on," I tell him. My face is a tall clear glass. Pour in your story, it says.

"The night of the drive to The City, that's where it ends and begins," Victor says quietly. "And all I was doing was going to see a chick. I felt good, the wind in my hair and the sunset a hot red, the big sky and my cool car and everything. We were going to hear music at one of those hip hotels on South Beach. Some band she liked, reggae. I remember her name but not her face. Usually it's the other way around."

I tighten the bathrobe belt at my waist. Victor asks, "Are you with me?" He doesn't wait for an answer but continues to talk. "At first I thought the trip itself had something to do with it. But I could never figure out how I went wrong. Driving down I-95, there are just so many wrong turns you can make. And none of them end up here."

Weak sunlight is filtering in the window behind Victor's head. This gives him a bit of a halo effect. The God upstairs.

"It has to do with who you are, who we are," Victor says. His fantasy seems to include me somehow. Again, there is nothing special in that. He's not special. A man like other men. "All of the cells in our bodies replace themselves constantly. So doesn't that indicate the opportunities we have for change? You and I," he says with a chin nod, "we were not always who we are now."

He waits for a response so I agree with him. Of course, he is correct. But that doesn't make him sane.

I have a better understanding of Victor now. I believe he is a Stage IV SIPD resident with a psychology background. A resident with brains and pull, with connections. I had better stay on his good side. And get into some clothes.

"Do you smell cheese fries?" I ask him.

Victor begins to laugh. And then we are both laughing. I guess he thinks that makes us friends.

They all think that.

8.

Victor is an excellent cook. He prepares a simple meal of brown rice stir-fried with sliced vegetables, ginger, soy sauce, and garlic. He prepares black pepper tea and cheese toast.

We eat at a small pine table. The food is steaming and bountiful, like a magazine photo of the best take-out Asian food. But my appetite is small. I am distracted. I am uncomfortable being here like this in a borrowed robe. I really need to return to my office as soon as possible. The storm seems to be over, and I expect the Group meeting scheduled for tonight will not be canceled.

Victor consumes every morsel on his plate. Then he reaches across the table for mine. "You mind?" he asks, then shovels in the rest of my food without waiting for a response. I watch him eat. He eats like a person in full recovery mode.

"I'm on the far side of all that," Victor says, as if he could read my mind. He wipes his nice lips with a paper napkin. "And once you catch up to where I'm at, we can work on things together. But you have to take a good look around you and begin to really see what is there. And what is not."

I stand up from the table and thank him for the meal, the coffee, the rescue. Victor waves it all away. Then he stands up and looks me in the eyes. He is at least six feet tall and rugged. Victor is appealing in many ways. So I let him place his hands on my shoulders and I look right back at him.

"If you lose what you think of as your self," Victor says slowly and quietly as if speaking to a child, "the dream becomes illogical, discontinuous. Yet the dream continues, the dream in which you are both subject and object, storyteller and characters in the story. If you lose your self to someone else, what then? Then they give you a new dream." He grins that wolfish smile I find myself liking more and more. "Oh, we all do this to different extents, we all entrust parts of our personality to the world around us. We start to dream others' dreams and we don't even know we're doing it. But if you realize that most of the information reaching you has been, how can I say this, *prearranged*? If you understand that what you are experiencing now is *not real*? Eventually you will begin to see."

When he lets go of my shoulders I can still feel the warmth of his large hands. His mind is not in full recovery mode, that's for sure.

A flock of monk parakeets squawk loudly as they stream by overhead. Late afternoon sun fills Victor's apartment and the pile of clothes steams in the heat. I pick up my wet skirt, blouse, hose and drape them over one arm.

"I'll return the robe clean and dry," I say on my way out the front door.

"Be smart, not slick," says Victor.

Ice drips down my spine and I shiver. His use of this simple expression strikes me as an odd coincidence. But surely, Franny was not the only person to use this particular phrase?

There is no one in the hall. All the doors are closed. I slip down the uncarpeted stairs to my office.

My door is unlocked. The office looks bleak compared to Victor's place. An Office Depot desk and rolling chair, the butterscotch couch, a small white bathroom. Functional at best.

In the bathroom, I drape my wet clothes over the shower curtain rod and set the damp pumps in the white tub. I keep spare clothes in the bathroom closet for emergencies like this, so I change into my work uniform of straight dark skirt, simple white blouse and beige hose. I feel back in control once more.

Time for a walk. I pull my Nike walking shoes out of the bottom of the closet and put them on. Then I stand at the window behind my desk. After-storm sunshine lights up the quad. I can almost see the deepest puddles shrinking. Soon they will be the absence of puddles. The absence of the aftermath of a forgettable storm. A storm like any other storm.

I glance up at my ceiling. The galaxy of stains appears to be located in the spot where, upstairs, we had piled our wet clothing on Victor's carpet. Where our raincoats and shoes formed a puddle. But how can that be? The stain was there when Justin was here, before we soaked the floor with our discarded clothing.

Time is passing in strange new ways.

I watch the people meandering along the sidewalks below. Stray residents and one or two employees cross and crisscross the damp and glistening quad. Everything glows pink and gold in the slant of the sinking sun.

Machinery whines in the distance. Beyond the quad, I locate the source of the drone: a tiny blue speck. Past the kiosk and the café, down the dirt drive to the entry gates, the faraway man in the blue uniform uses a chain saw. The lawn guy is cutting up some of the felled branches from the afternoon storm.

I am thinking about Victor, the way his overlapped teeth stood out white and clean in the afternoon light, the fresh lime smell of his skin, the old coin taste of his blood. His perfect dark roast coffee, the simple meal. His warm hands on my shoulders, his gaze gliding up and down my legs like a soft tongue. *Your cognition is a dream, a hallucination.*

Maybe so, but I should be concerned about my behavior this afternoon. It was way too personal and certain boundaries were crossed. This kind of behavior is widely regarded as unprofessional and I could easily lose my position here. Easily.

But okay, I admit it. I feel something for Victor.

You do a good job, you fuck up. It happens.

The greasy fast food smell of cheese fries wafts into the room. Ugh. I close the window and grab my keys from the cut-glass candy dish on my desk.

This time I lock the door behind me before I head down the stairs.

9.

Anders watches her come down the front drive. He likes the way she walks, rapid fire and with single-minded purpose. She stares straight ahead and Anders feels as if she is looking directly at him.

He slips behind the ficus hedge and waits until he thinks she has passed by.

She's gone through the open gate and is heading toward the beach. Anders wants to follow her there again today, but he has too much work to do. The storm knocked down many branches and it is his job to clean up all the debris. To cut all the wood and stack it for the refuse trucks to pick up outside the main entrance. He has to accomplish this task before dark. There is not enough time to follow the woman on her walk today.

It is Wednesday, his day off. Usually on Wednesdays he is able to follow her. But today, because of the tropical storm, he must work instead.

With a sigh, Anders picks up the chain saw and turns to the oak branch before him.

Later, while he stacks up the fresh cut wood, Anders thinks about the woman. The way she was with the resident, the big guy with the stupid smile on his face. How he put his arm around her and she let him.

Anders carries the wood a few feet to the handcart. The woman lets the sick people touch her. Anders knows he could not do this. He would have to change so much to be able to do it. He would have to be her, to wear her face and body, to walk to the sea in small white sneakers, to talk to the sick people in front of a window facing east.

Anders pushes the handcart full of cut wood toward the trailer he has hooked up to the mower. He's not sure he would want to do these things. Then he imagines himself brushing long blonde hair in front of a full-length mirror.

He dumps the pile of wood into the bigger pile in the trailer. Tonight she goes to the Burdome Building at seven o'clock. He has to hurry and finish cutting and hauling all the branches if he wants to have time for dinner first.

Wednesday is the best day of the week.

Anders starts up the mower and drives it slowly across the grounds, towing the trailer of fresh-cut wood. The fat on his belly jiggles and shakes as he rolls across the smooth damp grass. When he passes the windows of the residents' dining hall, he waves to the people inside. One of the dorm advisors waves back.

Anders can see that it is Joe. He likes Joe. Of all the dorm advisors, Anders likes Joe the best. Joe sits at a crowded table. He holds up a half-eaten cheeseburger and points to it. Anders laughs and continues on his way.

10.

I cross the empty street to the sidewalk on the north side. All the lawns I am passing are perfectly landscaped and obsessively manicured. Give a rich man a big empty yard and he will fool with it endlessly. He will fill it up with shrubs and annuals, trees and vines, he will fuck with it and blow money on it like it is a hot mistress. This is unhealthy for the man and for the planet.

I walk fast. When I take a good hard walk I always sleep more deeply. The deeper the sleep, the less likely I'll have nightmares.

There is no escaping your dreams, of course. Just like there is no escaping your life. If life is just a big long dream you cannot wake up from, dreams are short little versions of that. At least waking up from dreams is an option. But it is not always so simple. Sometimes you wake up with SIPD. Sometimes you cannot wake yourself up.

I can smell the salt before I am able to hear the pounding surf. The beach reeks of exposed clam beds today, of brine and seaweed, of iodine spilled on wind-raked sand. I cross the empty two-lane highway and follow the mulch path to the public rest rooms. There is a bench there, a bench made from recycled plastic milk bottles, where I can sit to remove my sneakers. And strip off my hose.

I leave my shoes under the bench. I tuck the pantyhose in one of the sneakers and scan the shoreline. No one on the beach, not a soul as far as I can see.

I walk from the rest rooms onto the rain-pocked sand, hiking past the lifeguard station. The tall wood chair with the red and white cross sits empty today. The tropical wave has scared off beach-goers. The surf is rough, tall frothy waves roaring in, scraping themselves back out again. But farther down the beach, I spot storm surfers. Four lean-bodied wetsuits, braving the thrash of the ocean. I stand and watch as the boys spring up, deftly manipulating their slippery boards. Sometimes they have control and sometimes they don't.

If you believe the current statistics, one out of the four will end up with SIPD. He will lose interest in surfing, and his friends will abandon him. He will fade away and so will the memories of gold and pink afternoons on a windswept beach with the wild waves and the laughter of those who share his special passion. A passion for being in the natural world, for becoming a part of it.

Hundreds of quivery see-through jellyfish the size of small saucers have been tossed up by the sea. The waves are white tipped and surly. Brown pelicans draft above me, then dive-bomb the fish. The air is so cool and clean I want to drink it. I walk and walk.

By the time I return to the lifeguard post the sun has set and the first few stars glimmer in a darkening sky. I am tired but invigorated. When I reach under the bench, my Nikes are still there.

But my panty hose is not. I search around the rest room building, check the sand, peer in a bright orange trash canister. Nothing. The stockings are gone.

I walk quickly through the increasing darkness. The night wind is picking up scattered sea grape leaves and tossing them like Frisbees. Cicadas begin their sex-driven chirping from hidden perches in the pine trees and live oaks I pass under. I imagine the many iguanas on the branches above me, and the monk parakeets, blue jays and mockingbirds. A hidden world I am unable to see. Not only because of the night before my eyes, but because I am blind to what is all around me.

Suddenly, I am walking across the quad. Like in a movie or a dream, I have fast-forwarded to the next scene. It is almost seven o'clock and I am due at the Burdome Building for Group.

I do not have time to wonder how this just happened. Or what it means.

11.

On my way to the Burdome Building, I stop at the convenience kiosk in the quad for a bottle of Diet-Water. The teenage girl behind the counter only has eyes for the tiny television screen on her phone. She does not count out my change, simply handing over the coins while managing to avoid contact with my outstretched palm. We do not speak a single word to one another.

This is how it is now. This is, I am coming to understand, the way we are choosing to survive.

I unscrew the plastic cap and drink fast as I walk the final block back to work. A big gold moon has popped up from somewhere. It leers down at me. I am not so self-absorbed tonight that I fail to recognize the autumn harvest moon. It is difficult for me to believe that this sock-it-to-me neon-yellow rock is the same moon I saw last month, that retiring ghostly globe visible only after dark.

Of course it's the same moon, but with a different, more outrageous persona.

Before I enter the brightly lit lobby of the Burdome, I stop to toss my empty bottle in a trash recycle bin made from recycled yogurt cups. The green can is designed to resemble a saw palmetto. Why must everything be reassembled to look like something else? I take a deep breath, and push through the heavy glass door.

The Malaise Group meets in the first floor auditorium of the Burdome Building on Wednesday nights at seven. We meet for two hours of group discussion. This schedule is supposed to make the weekly therapy meeting convenient for those members who have day jobs. However, the truth is, most members no longer do any sort of traditional work. Yet most of the Malaise Group fail to show up.

It's not called the Malaise Group for nothing.

The coffee pot is full of fresh hot coffee and there are Oreos lounging in a perfect circle on a white enamel serving platter better suited to a generous side of roast beef. A stack of sad green plastic dinner plates towers over an abstract design of hot pink paper napkins, each neatly folded on the diagonal, arcing across the well-worn refreshment table. Sasha hovers here, her back to the door, fingers twitching as she arranges and rearranges the Diet-Sugar packets in their unbreakable plastic serving bowl.

I clear my throat and Sasha startles, the nervous marsh rabbit caught in the headlights. No one else is here, which doesn't surprise me. We may add a few stragglers before our session ends at nine, Group members discovered loitering by their dorm advisers and forced to make an appearance here. Or we may not.

There is never much of a turnout for the Malaise Group meetings. I try not to take the low head count personally.

"Shall we get started?" I say now to Sasha. I say this every week.

We turn our backs on Sasha's pop art arrangement of coffee and cookies and napkins, and I lead her down the carpeted aisle to the soft-lit stage. As usual, a dozen uncomfortable metal folding chairs are set up onstage in a tight circle. Sasha follows me up the narrow stairs. We choose chairs spaced far apart, facing one another. When I drag my chair a few feet closer to hers, Sasha leans so far back that she tips at a dangerous angle.

"Okay," I say, as always. "Shall we begin?"

Sasha stares at her feet, thin paper flowers at the end of the pale stalks of her legs. Her chair teeters, her fingers wriggling on their willowy branches in the warm, slightly dusty auditorium air. She sprouts and droops, silent and empty.

After a day like today, I am having difficulty focusing on my work here tonight. And my legs are cold. I want to tuck them under me on a puffy couch in a cozy room. I want Victor's bathrobe soft and warm against my skin.

My mind lurches, veering down various paths. Sasha sits and stares at her wriggle of fingers, thinking her own incomprehensible thoughts.

I am wondering if it is strange that Victor speaks in Franny's words. I am wondering if it is strange that Justin had an old photo of me. I am wondering if it is strange that Celia with her crumpled up skin and thin clown hair has dreams similar to my own. I am wondering how I got to this point. The point where my work feels distant and hopeless, my life empty and distant. My mind races backward in time, rehashing for me how busy I kept it throughout the decades of schooling, the years of classes and clinics and study. All that time and effort, for what? So I can sit around with people who care even less than I do about what it all means? Where did I lose the path to meaning?

I do not struggle with my mind. It seems pointless. I let it ramble off, seeking its own way.

My legs shiver until the knee bones knock together. I am breathing in the dust of last Wednesday night, and all the Wednesdays before that one. The weekly Group meetings here line up in my mind's eye. The nights on this folding chair stretch back in time to a distant pinpoint of light. To the vanishing point. I let my mind travel toward the tiny spark of light at the beginning of all that I know now.

The prisoner awakens.

"Sasha?" I prod. She stares at her fingers as if they are a psychedelic slideshow in her lap, where they flutter and weave themselves into shapes, then grip one another and collapse in a heap on her thighs. Sasha's long black hair is stringy. It hangs in her narrow face. She rarely talks in Group. Even when the group consists of just the two of us.

Another silent Wednesday night. The row of silent nights stretches on into the future without an end in sight. I feel my life drifting away, one silent Wednesday night at a time.

A door slams at the back of the room and a young man saunters in. He reeks of beer. It is a sign of mental wellness that he is actively drinking and, possibly, partying like nonresidents do. His hair is short and white blonde, his tan the kind that signifies good health rather than vanity. I doubt this boy in his clean jeans and bright blue T-shirt is a resident looking to join the Malaise Group.

He waves at us and pours himself a coffee, then fills a plate with cookies. He whistles a tune that sounds vaguely hard rock, vaguely familiar. His buoyancy is remarkable, even if it is alcohol induced. It's refreshing.

The young guy approaches the stage with hands full, bounds up the stairs without dropping anything, and sits down next to Sasha. He is tall and lanky but muscular, well-built. He is good looking too, with a bashful smile. He does not seem to notice when Sasha carefully leans her body as far away from his as she is able to without scooting her chair. I am watching Sasha tip precariously.

"Sasha, sit up straight, please," I say. She ignores me and continues to lean dangerously.

She should be leaning in the other direction. A healthy young woman would be tipping her body toward this cute boy, a fetching smile on her face. Sasha has no sex drive, however. She expresses so little vital energy that I see her body as an empty container. Motivated by a wounded animal's instinct to withdraw, she tips her chair as far back as it can go.

Like most of the residents here who I am at a loss to help, I myself have not indulged lately in good, hard, rollicking and rolling sex. Not for a long time. They may have SIPD, I have no viable men in my life. I cannot remember the last time I had memorable sex.

Perhaps this is what Victor has picked up on, this yawning absence in me. Like the missing dough in the center of a bagel.

"Hey, I guess you're in charge here," the blond boy says to me. He is wolfing a cookie. When I smile, he leans toward me, his breath beery sweet. "I'm Ben. I go to the U and I'm majoring in psychology. My prof told me to come, he said we should come on a Wednesday evening and sit in on the Malaise Group. To get a feel for the disorder. SIPD."

The boy smiles and swigs his coffee. We look nakedly at one another while Sasha slowly steadies herself, returning the chair to safe balance on all four of its skinny legs.

I am wondering how old he is and what it feels like to be inside his head. His mind is still open, innocent of the horrors of SIPD. His mind is still free. (But really, what kind of mind is *free*?) Before I can get my act together and say something intelligent, however, Sasha beats me to it.

"Do you have dreams while awake, dreams you are unable to awaken from?" Sasha says in her soft voice. She regards her own lap where the bony knees under her rumpled skirt protrude and quake. "This is SIPD Stage I. Do you lose track of yourself? Do you have to struggle to maintain your vigilance? This is SIPD Stage II."

I watch Ben and he gazes serenely at Sasha. He continues to eat Oreos, occasionally gulping coffee. How long has it been since I ate cookies with abandon? Since I did anything with a sense of abandon?

When I was seventeen my boyfriend raped me when we were kissing on the beach at low tide. Before that night, he had rarely touched my bare skin. In public, he would not put an arm around my shoulder or hold my hand. But that hot June night, he just had to have me. He couldn't *not* have me. His bony sternum poked hard against my small breasts, his broad back covered in sweat and sand. I remember scratching him in the face, the eyes. Our sex was, I would learn later, rough sex. That first time was rape, but after that I often initiated. We continued on in this way, our angry passion fueling a deep need to hurt one another, until we both went off to college.

"Do you find your mind has fallen away into a state of randomness? This is SIPD Stage III," recites Sasha. She moves on to list the symptoms. "Symptom One: You begin to feel like you do not care about your life anymore. Two: You *really* don't care anymore."

As I watch Ben eat, I lick my lips as if they were studded with crumbs.

Why am I thinking about my old boyfriend? And rough sex? The prisoner has swallowed the key, is what I find myself thinking. The prisoner has swallowed the key.

I need to collect myself and refocus. As much as I hate to stop her, I must interrupt Sasha. It is my job to guide the group in the proper direction.

"Ben." I like the way his little baby name rests softly on my tongue. "Do you have a letter of introduction from your professor? A visitor's pass from the reception desk?"

His blue green eyes are wide and clear, and staring into them is relaxing, like a bath in the summer sea. But I see a disturbance there, a ripple coming toward me, and he looks away.

A door at the back of the auditorium opens and one of our dorm advisors steps inside. Joe is a big man (they all are), dressed in the standard-issue whites, with a heavy belt and its prerequisite tangle of keys jingling from his super-size-me waist. Joe does not smile or call to us, but he waves an acknowledgment.

Behind him, a second man of even larger dimensions steps into the auditorium. His blue uniform stretches across a middle-aged burst of a gut, but his face is young. And blank.

It's the young man who mows the lawn. He is staring directly at me, so I smile politely. His face is as round and expressionless as the moon. No wonder I never have sex anymore. All day and into the night I am surrounded by men who are residents and men who should be residents but are not.

I smell cheese fries again.

Both men leave, as suddenly and silently as they arrived.

Ben swears under his breath and Sasha laughs. She laughs! This could be seen as a Malaise Group miracle. No one ever laughs in Group. Remember, the people here do not care about anything. They barely care enough to show up. And Sasha, a twenty-one-year-old child, has lived here since her junior year in high school. Sasha has not matured, she's frozen emotionally at age sixteen. Clinically, she is a Stage III sleepwalker with a medical file thicker than a dictionary. Yet here she is, laughing with a young man her own age. Like a normal girl.

Ben grins at us. He has a dimple in the center of his chin.

"Let's continue," I suggest and Ben nods.

Then Sasha nods. This too is like a little miracle. Sasha is actively participating in Group. Sasha regularly attends the Malaise Group, and every week she lines up the food, the napkins and the sugar packets. But she isn't really there.

This is what SIPD is all about.

"Symptom Three: Your memories from when you cared about your life become twisted and ugly," she says. "You remember things that didn't happen, violent things, weirdly distorted events. Symptom Four: You lose affect, weight, muscle tone and skin color. You have become lost in the false world inside your own head."

My mouth is dry as I ask Ben if he is already familiar with the stages and symptoms of Stand-in Personality Disorder. Or does he wish for Sasha to continue to provide our newcomers' welcome information? I am ignoring proper clinical procedure and institutional bylaws here. He has no letter of introduction, no pass from Administration. But he is demonstrating a certain power, eliciting a restorative effect on a Group member. His eyebrows are auburn and perfectly shaped.

Ben says, "Here's what I know. Stage IV is when you begin to feel like someone else is living your life. At this point, all your symptoms improve. Because it's as if someone else is in your body now and they're living through your physical being. I mean, that's how it feels to the person with Stage IV Stand-in Personality Disorder."

He has finished his plate of cookies and he places it carefully on the floor next to his chair. "From what I've read, there's a number of viable medications available for treating people with SIPD," he says. "Like Adjuster, I mean. And derivatives, the generics. But these drugs only quiet the symptoms while failing to cure the disorder." He pauses, hesitating. "Although it *is* curable. At least, that's what they taught us in psyche class."

I can smell the advancing tide. I used to like to bite my high school boyfriend's exposed flesh while we rolled across damp sand toward the tide line. Sometimes he held my head under the rise of the waves until I came up spluttering.

"Do you feel frightened of SIPD?" Sasha's reedy voice brings me back to the stage lights, to Group. "Do you worry you will come down with the disorder, or are you afraid you might already have it? Does anyone in your family suffer from SIPD? Have they been institutionalized?" Sasha is listing the warning signs of SIPD. She has two hospital green plates of cookies. She hands one to me, taking an Oreo for herself from the other plate before passing it on to Ben.

I rest the plate in my lap. A pink paper napkin, a hot pink triangle, perches on its knees in the center of the plate. Five black and white cookies are arranged in a circle around the napkin.

The prisoner has swallowed the key, my mind informs me once more, this time from what seems like a great distance away.

"Randomness," Ben says.

I am thinking how much better it would be inside Ben's body instead of my own. I am not craving him as a sexual object, I do not want him inside me, not like that. No, what I am thinking about is how very fine life would be if it were me inside him. What if I were looking out at the world through those innocent, sugar-glazed, beer-blurred eyes? Seeing life like a six-pack of cold beer or a tray of cookies laid out for my personal enjoyment, an enjoyment I constantly indulged. Seeing life through the buzz of carefree day after day of mindless college classes in which wizened profs promise there are cures for everything, solutions for all the woes of the world. A world I was not in any hurry to join.

"I'm interested in the pathology of SIPD," Ben explains. "And I'm not afraid of the disorder."

Like seeks like, I am thinking. He is nothing, he is important, he is a man like all men, a man who feels superior simply for being a man. And me, I am a smart girl. I can figure it all out myself.

"There's a sense of deep randomness," Ben says. "I mean, something's seriously off." He pauses and looks at me for a brief but intense moment. I feel something hard and cold lodged in the back of my throat. "This is what it has come to. Everybody knows it."

Sasha and I nod. We wait quietly, balancing our plates on our thin white thighs.

12.

Anders waits outside the Burdome Building in the bright moonlight. The wind is sweet and smooth now. All the dark clouds from the afternoon storm have scattered and disappeared. This happens every time, and each time Anders enjoys the refreshing coolness that follows a tropical wave. Tonight is especially nice because the moon has come up big and yellow and round as the sun.

Anders likes a full moon. He can feel the liquids inside his body welling up. His blood swishes around and he hears a pulsing in his ears. He rides that tide like a surfer dude. But sometimes he feels as if his head is underwater on the nights when the moon is full.

He stands behind the recycling can by the front door, leaning against the brick building and waiting patiently for the woman to come out. Joe went off to do rounds. Before he left, Joe said to meet him later, over at the gym, and Anders said okay, he would be there. But first he wants to follow the woman when she walks back to her own building. Then he wants to sit on his favorite bench in the quad to stare at her window until her light comes on.

After that, Anders will go to the gym and hang out with the guys. Hours later, when he comes back to the bench in the quad, the light in the woman's window will be off. Then Anders will go home to his apartment in The City and sleep.

In general, Anders knows he is not good with time. Time bends and wobbles, stretching itself out and falling back on itself. Time is not to be trusted, Anders thinks. That's why he likes his routines. His dull, comforting routines.

But things are changing. *He's* changing.

Like tonight. Tonight, for the first time ever, he stepped inside the Burdome Building. Joe is allowed to go inside on his rounds, to check on locks and shut off lights, but Anders is not. Anders has no business inside the Burdome Building. So he is worried that he has made a serious mistake and will get in trouble with Administration.

Joe said don't worry about it, but Anders is upset. Anders' knees are shaking a little.

He squats down behind the recycling bin to still his shivering legs.

Anders talks quietly to himself. He tells himself everything will be okay and nobody will care what he has done tonight. But, he warns himself, he cannot go inside the Burdome Building again. No trespassing! He has been told not to do this and he won't. Not anymore. And he certainly will not go into the woman's building. He cannot follow her to her place and wait until she has gone inside and then force open the front door to her building and go inside and go up the stairs to her door and force that one open and go into her room and stare at her close up. Like he wants to do. No, he cannot do this. No, Anders tells himself over and over, I will not do this.

But he really wants to do this.

The fluid inside Ander's head throbs and the liquid from his brain begins to drip from his nose and eyes. Is he crying? Anders is not sure. All he knows is how much he wants to touch the woman's long blonde hair and maybe her skirt, the skirt that flies up in the wind. That's all. Just touch her hair and her skirt.

But Anders knows this is not all he wants to do.

Anders wants to keep on doing a good job. That's most important. But what Anders also wants to do is touch what he's not supposed to touch. He wants to touch because he wants to know. To know what it feels like to be soft and gentle and flowerlike and blonde and wet in the rain and under a skirt that changes color because it gets wet and it flies up in the wind and it comes off. It comes off and becomes something else because it is no longer there. He wants to touch what can change so he can change too.

The moon pulls at the blood rushing around inside Anders and the water from his head drips out a little at a time until he feels emptied and hollow. He continues to squat behind the can that looks like a palm tree, waiting. He waits for the woman to come out of the building.

He waits for whatever will happen next.

13.

"Ever since my teens I've had these random desires. Almost like compulsions, but not quite," Ben is telling them. He has stopped gobbling cookies and slurping coffee and sits hunched forward in his chair. Sasha is sitting forward too. So am I.

"Everyone has them," reassures Sasha. I nod in agreement.

Here we are, three people sharing feelings, opening up. We are practically putting our heads together. This is what the Malaise Group is supposed to be all about but never is.

"I know. That's why I'm here," says Ben. "I want to know what it all means. And why it's all getting so much worse now. Like for me. I mean, now I've developed this really weird desire, or like a compulsion that is super focused." He pauses, looks down at his plate. "Okay, well, right now I'm totally focusing on the number one hundred and eleven."

His eyes dart back and forth. Sasha and I say nothing.

"I mean, when I feel stressed or out of it, or if I wake up after a certain kind of dream, or sometimes if I just let my mind wander, it happens. The urge happens. And no matter where I am or what I'm doing, no matter what time it is or even if it's the middle of the night, I have to go. I have to go out and find it. I have to go out and walk and walk and walk. Until I find it. Until I actually see the number. The number one hundred and eleven, I mean." Ben holds up his hands as if to say, *don't shoot.* "I'll leave my class or a party or my job or my dorm and I'll walk and walk. I'll keep walking until I see it on a mailbox or an apartment building or a billboard or a menu for an all-night restaurant. Until I finally see the number one hundred and eleven I just keep walking. But then I see it and the super focused, hard-driving desire just dies right down and the compulsion fades and I heave a huge sigh of relief. Then I just turn around and go back to school or work or the dorm." He shakes his head, smiles. "And I feel good. After."

Ben looks hard at Sasha, then at me. He is trusting us with this information.

"I mean, I go crazy looking for my number, then I find it and I feel an inner release and I can relax again. I know this is strange but I don't think I'm losing it. I mean, I'm not developing a personality disorder, am I?" He shrugs, glances at me, then away. "I sleep real well and my dreams stay in their own reality, my dreams don't merge with my life. And I care about things. I care about school and my job at the bar and looking good and all that." Ben blushes. "I mean, I'm just telling you why I'm interested in psychology and mental disorders." He laughs, obviously uncomfortable.

"You probably have a mild stress-induced obsession," I tell him. "It's like a tic, a nervous tic. But, for you, seeing a certain number rather than making a specific body movement relieves the stress." My voice is gentle, reassuring. "This kind of ritualized behavior is not uncommon these days. But even if your compulsion magnifies, even if you begin to develop an Obsessive Compulsive Disorder, this is not necessarily a stepping stone to SIPD."

Ben is fortunate. He is still one of the healthy ones.

"Maybe. But what's with the randomness?" Ben asks. "Everyone knows the randomness is getting worse. I mean everyone's talking about it. And what's with the number one hundred and eleven? I've been obsessed with girls in the past and, well, other stuff. More normal stuff. But a number? Don't you think that's like really weird?"

"You've come to the wrong place if you're looking for someone to tell you your behavior is weird," volunteers Sasha. She has tiny smile wrinkles at the corners of her small dark eyes. "At least you're able to handle school and a job, and you have a normal life. That counts for something."

"I guess," admits Ben. "So you don't think this is leading to a loss of personality." He rubs his nose with one finger and frowns. "That's a relief. But still. I *am* behaving like a weirdo. No offense," Ben says to Sasha.

I sit back in my chair and watch. Let the young people work on their issues together.

"I mean, I didn't come here to talk about myself or say anything bad about people with SIPD. You do have SIPD, right?" Ben asks Sasha and she nods. They stare into one another's eyes.

Maybe they can feel something. Together.

I half-listen while they talk. What I don't do is share my thoughts on Ben's so-called random compulsion.

90

Because I am not so sure it *is* random. Because my office number is one hundred and eleven.

"At least you're out in the world. Even if it's a struggle to keep it together," Sasha says.

Ben smiles. "Life out in the big world isn't all that wonderful. Especially these days."

"That's probably true," Sasha says. "But it *is* living. Living your life, rather than avoiding it or escaping it. Be grateful you can leave here tonight and never come back. If you choose not to."

Ben looks at Sasha and cocks his head. "Nobody said anything when I walked in here tonight. So, what would happen if we were to leave here right now? Who would stop us? Those big, dumb-looking guys who stopped in here for a minute?"

"No, Ben, it's not like that," I explain. "There are no locked gates and no guards on duty at the front entrance. In fact, the front gate is never locked. That gate stands open day and night. Residents can come and go as they wish. But most stay right here. They no longer feel safe out in the world, so they stay put."

The prisoners have swallowed the keys.

Ben leaps up with a grin. "Of course it's not safe out there. So let's go!" His voice is excited and he waves his arms. "I mean, I've got to go. I need to go look for my number. Talking about it has sparked the urge. Maybe you two want to come along?"

He looks down at Sasha hopefully, his hair a shock of white in the stage lights, his tan face lit with the kind of hopeful expectancy I once had. The kind of passion I would do anything to have again.

"When I gotta go, I gotta go," Ben says with a shrug. "But I'd love you guys to come along. And see what I'm talking about here. Tell me what you think is going on," he says as he begins to walk backward toward the stairs.

Sasha shakes her head. She looks sad. This too is progress. At least she is expressing some feeling. "Sorry, Ben," she says. "I'll have to take a rain check."

Sometimes certain steps must be taken, specific things must be completed, before anybody is ready to listen. I will not tell Ben about the number on my office door, but I will go with him while he walks the streets looking for his number. Looking for a random one hundred and eleven.

"Okay, Ben," I call out to him as I stand and stretch. "I just happen to have my walking shoes on tonight," I say as I head down the stairs after him and Sasha. "And it looks like this week's Malaise Group meeting is over."

14.

We stand in front of the Burdome Building in a splash of white-gold moonlight. Sasha and Ben are still talking and the wind is whipping their hair gently like a paddle fan on low and the cicadas are chirping from the oak trees where they must be mating or looking to mate and for some reason everything is starting to speed up. I hold my hands up to my face and I can see right through the milky skin to the bones. The bones in my hands are like twigs, I think, little helpless twigs trembling in an evening breeze.

Sasha leaves with a casual, over the shoulder wave. The darkness eats her in a few bites, and I am alone with Ben on the sidewalk. I let my hands fall to my sides and ask, "Now what?"

Ben touches my shoulder lightly and smiles. His dimple is like a hole in his chin in the black and white photo we make in the darkness. "Now we go straight to some random but perfectly placed one hundred and eleven. And then we have few drinks and you tell me what you think," he says.

Sounds like bar therapy, is what I am thinking. I smile and nod. A man like all men. Nothing I can't handle.

There is an odor on the wind that is unpleasant. Familiar. Meaty and slightly rank.

I link my arm through Ben's and say, "Let's go."

It feels nice to touch his body, his biceps wonderfully solid and warm. Like a smooth stone at rest in the sun. I would like to have such muscles, men's muscles that are well defined and strong. As we stroll through the silent quad, in and out of the yellow pools of light cast by street lamps, I am thinking how interesting it would be to walk around in a male body, looking out at the world through a man's eyes.

Ben picks up the pace. He is tall and his legs are long, but so are mine. To match Ben's gait, I must let go of his arm.

"Do you smell cheese fries?" I ask.

He slows his pace, tilts his head back and sniffs the air. "You know, I do smell fast food," he says. "Is there a dining hall around?"

"This is the central quad we are crossing right now," I explain, and launch into a brief version of our visitor's tour. "The center has a total of twenty buildings including residential dorms, a cafeteria and outdoor café, the residents' dining hall, several office buildings, the gym, and an inpatient hospital. We have outpatient facilities too, but most of these are located in The City."

"On Second Street, right? I've walked past the outpatient housing and the therapy center many times. One benefit of my compulsion is I know this town like the back of my hand. Better, probably, even though I am quite familiar with the back of my hand." Ben laughs. He pauses. "I didn't want to say anything in Group tonight, but I've seen you before. On my walks. I've seen you out walking too. Many times," he says without looking at my face or slowing his stride. "Hope that's not too freaky."

"What do you mean, freaky?" I ask. A cold shudder passes through my rib cage. I do not like to be spied on. Or watched by unseen eyes. Even the thought of being stalked evokes a chilly paranoia.

"I mean, I didn't come to the Malaise Group tonight to look for you or anything. It's not like I knew you'd be there. It's just a coincidence. Okay? I don't want you to think I'm a stalker."

My high school boyfriend used to stalk me, although we did not call it that. It was part of our game, our rough sex game, and I was into it as much as he was. At least, I believed I was at the time. Maybe I just didn't know any better. Either way, I allowed it to happen and, at the time, it excited me.

In one version of the game we played, he would wait for me outside my family's house. As I lay on my bed on a school night, reading Twain or studying algebra, I would begin to feel his presence. I would get so excited. I wanted him so much on those nights.

When I snuck out to find my boyfriend, my brothers would cover for me. All three of my brothers encouraged me to rebel in small ways against the rigid confines of my parents' conservative rule of law. My brothers must have thought I went out to smoke dope and drink a few beers. They were normal boys with fast cars and hot girlfriends and multiple school detentions. All of the negative attention was centered on them. They thought it was healthy for me to stand up for myself too.

But really, that was not what I was doing. I was not standing up for anyone at all.

My brothers never would have let me out of the house if they had known about the games I was playing with my high school boyfriend. They never imagined their little sister wandering around in the dark, removing her clothes. They would have killed my boyfriend if they ever found out how he waited all those times in our yard, how he lay there in the black night beneath the wind-tossed fishtail palms, waiting for me to undress. How he always grabbed me from behind, clasping a dirty hand over my mouth and pulling me to the ground.

One time I got the upper hand and roped my boyfriend to a big banyan tree. I used his thin undershirt, cramming it in his mouth so he couldn't yell at me. My thighs were pulsing that night with the feeling a woman gets when she owns a man.

Boys all had the body I wanted. Not to hold onto in pleasure or pain, not to enfold and merge with my own, but to replace my own. To take the place of my body. To change me into someone else.

After that one time, however, my high school boyfriend was more careful to maintain control. He would wait for me in my back yard, then drag me down the street to where he parked his parents' Buick. Sometimes he drove us to the beach for a struggle down by the tide line. Other times we just fooled around in the back seat. Almost like any other teenage couple. Except I would be left with the marks his hands made on my skin.

He liked to wrap his big cold hands around my throat. He liked that a lot. It scared me to feel the extent of the physical power he had over me. The physical and sexual and emotional power he was able to wield. It scared me and it excited and confused me and we went on like that until we both went off to college.

Ben is quiet, peering through the darkness as we hike past the brightly lit mansions set along the road like cupcakes on black velvet. He stops only to check the house numbers on the mailboxes. None have the number we seek.

"That last mailbox was fourteen-fifty, and the numbers are going up." Ben increases the pace sharply. "We need to be in The City. The numbers are too limited way out here. And there are no cars. So no license plates."

As he speeds up I drop back, following along at an increasing distance. I am tiring and losing all sense of connectedness in the warm black night. The moon has moved to a new position behind us and appears dimmer, less golden, less sparkly than it did earlier. A more restrained persona, perhaps?

I walk slow and try to catch my breath. I do not feel well. I might have to say I do not feel myself. I want to take off all my clothes and lie down on one of these cool green lawns. I want to lie back in the grassy hand of some unseen stranger.

My brain is fogging over as random thoughts push their way into my mind. Almost like snatches of dreams, little wisps of images and brief scenes from my life. Only, the memories seem created, like they may be memories from someone else's life.

I am thinking about or dreaming of or watching a young woman with long blonde hair and clear green eyes. She serves drinks, she talks and laughs as she moves rapidly and gracefully, working her way up and down a mahogany bar. Her reflection in the mirror above the bar leans forward as she listens to an old guy in a leather jacket slumped on a bar stool. She smiles and pats the man on the shoulder. She hands a drink to a talkative woman wearing a brightly colored head scarf, then fills a pitcher with beer from a tap, pumping slowly enough to allow the perfect head to form.

As these images flicker across the landscape of my mind, I walk slower and slower, trying to make sense of them. The more I imagine or dream or watch the bartender, who is some version of me, the more it seems like she is the one who is real. I am beginning to feel as if the woman in my head is the real me. And the woman imagining her, the woman trailing Ben through the night and gradually falling behind, that woman is *not* me.

Like the dream me is real, but the person doing the dreaming is not.

The dream continuity in my mind offers me an existence in which I belong and am featured. I can feel the pulse of it, the heat of that existence. It calls to me like a lover. Then the images blink off.

I bump into Ben. He is standing in the center of the narrow sidewalk staring over my head. His body is taut and he grabs me hard when I yelp in surprise.

"Shhhh!" he warns, clasping a hand across my mouth.

I start to choke and gasp.

He lets go. "Sorry. But be quiet for a minute. I think someone is following us." He's whispering.

All I can think about is how every life story has an unhappy ending. Because they all end the same way, with the storyteller dead to this world.

15.

The woman looks right at Anders. She doesn't seem to see him, though.

A hawk swoops overhead. Anders watches the big bird circling, searching the park beside them for a mouse or a rat. Anders admires raptors. He admires how they see through the night to the object of their desire. He admires how these birds reach into the darkness to take what they want.

He can hear the woman talking now. "I do that too," she says. "Sometimes I imagine someone is following me. Especially when it's late like this. And like you said, no cars. Kind of creepy. The mind plays tricks."

Headlights poke through the darkness, bouncing off Anders' back to light up the couple ahead of him. He can see the woman's long smooth face, her fleshy lips and silky hair. She doesn't look at Anders, but watches as the car slowly passes. An old Ford Mustang, a car from an earlier time and place.

"Ben!" the woman calls out. "The license!"

Anders watches as the boy, Ben, lets go of the woman and raises both arms in the air. Like the car scored a touchdown. The woman laughs. It is the first time Anders has heard her laugh. She has a low throaty laugh. A coarse man's laugh. He wants to take that laugh and hold it in his fist.

The couple walk slowly into the park. They sit down together on a bench across from a children's swing set. All the plastic swing seats are empty and so lightweight they rock back and forth in the evening breeze.

He imagines cutting the tall boy down to size with his chain saw, slicing off limbs and tossing them in the handcart. Downsizing him. Changing him so he can't touch her anymore.

Anders would like to change the boy, Ben. He would like to change himself more, though.

Now Anders can't hear any of the words that are being spoken so he just watches as they talk quietly to one another, sitting close together on the park bench. The moonlight makes both of their bodies look speckled, glittery. Like sequins.

Neither of them says anything to Anders. He just stands there by himself on the edge of the park. Waiting for the woman and whatever future she might be creating for him. For all of them.

Go ahead, Anders thinks. Talk all you want.

16.

I find myself sitting with Ben on a small park bench made from recycled plastic Diet-Water bottles. Listening to Ben. Or not listening to Ben. Somehow, the scene has changed and time has passed in some abbreviated form.

"I was supposed to work tonight, and now I'm totally late," Ben is saying. "I like the bar job so I don't want to lose it. But it's only a temporary thing anyway, a means to an end. I don't see bartending as a career. Not for me anyway. Maybe owning a bar or a franchise, I can see that."

I can see chugging down a stiff one right now, is what I am thinking. Especially after a day like today. I would really enjoy a cold beer and a shot of Wild Turkey right about now. Oh yeah.

"Ben," I interrupt. "Didn't you say that after we found your number we would talk about things over a few drinks? So why don't we go to your bar?"

Ben likes the idea so we stand up and brush the bench dirt from our backsides, and I smooth down my skirt.

"How far is the bar from here?" I ask as we leave the park. The asphalt under our sneakered feet glistens in the sheen of the street lamps, but the puddles have disappeared. All the rainwater has been reclaimed, I am thinking. All that fresh water, used and reused without a drop wasted. The perfect system.

"It's downtown, a few blocks from the Second Street outpatient center," Ben says as he picks up speed. He glances at a clunky sports watch on his wrist. "It's only ten. My manager likes me, so maybe if I relieve her for the night she'll let things pass. I mean, I can't keep running off whenever I feel the urge. I certainly can't do this when I get a real job."

A few wispy clouds trail themselves through the moonlit sky. The breeze is mildly floral, sweetly caressing my skin. Ben chatters away, and I punctuate his monologue with the occasional noncommittal grunt.

He thinks this makes us friends. They all think that.

As we reach the outskirts of The City, we are greeted by unfurling waves of late-night clamor and the stench of tropical rot. We are ablaze in red and green neon and the sudden repetitive flash of oncoming headlights. Traffic appears as if out of nowhere. We are no longer alone with the night. We pass pulsating clots of activity on the sidewalk, mostly in the form of rowdy students spilling out of noisy bars and clubs.

I cannot remember the last time I went out for a memorable night on the town.

The false daylight of the city street creates a trance state for me that I stumble through readily. The air is vibrant, electric, and it smells like a mix of overripe pineapple, fresh vomit and spicy aftershave. Music escapes from dark storefront interiors, ear-pounding music, along with gunshot bursts of laughter.

We walk past Big Boy Bagel Deli. It's packed with students. Ben steers me through an open doorway into the dark barroom next door.

My eyes take a minute to adjust to the dim ale-colored lighting. Then I see her, moving around behind the mahogany bar. She stops to pour a generous shot of

Black Velvet for an older man slumped on a backless bar stool. When he sits up straight and reaches for his drink, she looks at us and frowns.

I am frowning too. And it is like looking in a mirror, a crazy funhouse mirror.

"Ben, Ben, Ben. What am I going to do with you?" the bartender asks, shaking her head.

Ben hurries to the bar.

"What would you do with you if you were me?" she says with a half-smile.

"I would give me that apron, then take the rest of the night off. That's what I would do if I were you," Ben says. He holds out an open hand and waggles his fingers. "Hand it over, Virginia. You know you want to go home and be with your man tonight. Let Bartender Ben take over for the evening," he teases.

I watch her face when her smile widens. Even her eyes smile. She has green eyes, Irish eyes, and a lot of pale blonde hair. "You are not me, Ben, but you can play me for the rest of the night. I'll take you up on that offer." She unties the strings of her long white butcher's apron. Then she looks over at me. "Who's your date?"

Are we really so different from one another?

Ben speaks softly and Virginia waves me over to the bar. She indicates an empty stool and says, "You can have a couple drinks on the house, honey. As long as you don't let this character run off before closing time."

Virginia points to Ben, then to a digital clock in an alcove above the long rows of brightly colored bar bottles. "See that he stays behind the bar until twelve-fifty. Then, after he clears out the room and closes up, *then* he can pull his disappearing act. Okay?"

"Okay," I say. I cannot take my eyes off her, Virginia looks so much like the woman in my bartender fantasy. She looks like me in that fantasy.

And now *she has a name.*

I am full of unanswered questions. I want to know all about her: where she comes from and where she lives now, how old she is, who the man is she is going home to, how long she has worked at the bar. Does she like her job? I want to ask her, do you *feel* for your life, *do you love your life?*

Ben is behind the bar now with the apron tied at his waist. Virginia talks to him about receipts, inventory, and which drunks have been kicked out for the night. Ben finally shushes her, gently pushing her toward the door to the back room.

When he turns around to begin taking orders, Virginia stands in the doorway. We look into one another's eyes. We look deeply, like lovers.

She turns and disappears into the back room.

When she is gone, I stare into the mirror over the bar. I am looking for Virginia, but I am only seeing myself.

How disappointing.

In the bar-length mirror I can see most of the room behind me. There are quite a few people in the bar for a Wednesday night, mostly young couples with their arms around each other and small groups of inebriated women in their twenties or early thirties. A few older men sit alone at the bar, drinking seriously. Professional drinkers, every good bar has them. There's an old Wurlitzer jukebox, which seems to be programmed to play rock 'n' roll oldies.

The ghost of Harry Chapin mourns the pitfalls of time passing until it has come full circle. Someone shatters a glass on the unswept floor. Ben looks up from juggling mugs out of the dishwasher and scowls. A woman hoots, one of those primal drunken laughs.

There is a mild and uncomfortable tickle in my throat. I cough and clear my throat several times. Ben places a foamy mug of beer in front of me and says, "Try this on for size."

So I do. And it fits perfectly. It fits so perfectly Ben quickly brings me another one. When I ask him for a shot of Wild Turkey, he lifts those fine auburn eyebrows.

"Sure?" he asks me, before complying with my request. "I'll drive you home later, then," he says while he sets up my boilermaker.

I cannot remember the last time I forgot everything after drinking too much.

Over my second beer, I dare to inquire about Virginia. Ben leans across the bar so that our heads almost touch. He is confiding in me again.

I am all ears.

"I love that woman," Ben admits. "She's fair and, like tonight, asks no questions. Because she likes me. *She allows for my weirdness.* I would quit obsessing and running off, just to make her proud of me. If I could."

When I ask where she's from, Ben shrugs. "Virginia doesn't talk about her life too much. But she's run this place for years. She lives outside The City with her partner, the man who owns this place. Guy named Vic. Cool guy, savvy and tough. Guy's loaded too. Nobody messes with Vic."

When I ask about Vic, Ben says, "He owns this whole block, including the deli," before moving down the bar to refill a pitcher for a plump young woman in a head scarf and flip-flops.

Virginia lives with Vic who owns the Big Boy Bagel Deli? Where the absence of dough makes the bagels what they are?

Is Virginia nothing, yet important? Is she by any chance important *to me?* Might her cognition be nothing but a dream, an elaborate hallucination? Her own, *or possibly mine?*

"Bartender," I call out. "Can I have another round over here?"

My mind has loosened from its tight collar and leash, and is beginning to wander freely around the back yard.

What kind of mind is *really* free?

"You want another shot, lady, or do you want to change your order?" Ben calls as he works his way back down the bar. He has a dish rag over one shoulder and his white hair shimmers in the fluorescence lighting up the bar bottles.

"I want to change my order," I say.

What I don't say is, I want to change *everything.*

17.

Anders doesn't like the downtown part of The City at night. But he bucks up, and stands tall outside the crowded bar. He peers in through the open door. After a while, he wanders around the side of the building to wait in the darkness of the alley there.

He squats down and rests. Anders' hands smell like gasoline and fresh-cut wood. His fingers are sticky with ficus and palm sap. His eyes and nose are dripping again. Maybe this is from inhaling gas fumes and tree sap, not from anything inside his heart, Anders thinks. Or maybe the woman is making him leak.

She has to move the story along, Anders says to himself. The clock over the bar does not tick, but time passes. Soon it will be too late.

Anders waits and waits, his mind a blank sheet. Finally he stands up slowly. He walks out of the alley and around to the front of the bar. Anders is thirsty. He wants something, he wants everything.

Anders looks inside. He can tell the woman has had too much alcohol. He knows that feeling, it has happened to him too. You feel separate from your body and your body feels real good. Before it begins to feel real bad, that is. But before that, the good feeling is in your body and in your head. Your heart feels light. Your mind is free of the problem of thinking about itself, and you feel like you want to push and push what is no longer there, hard and hard and harder.

When the woman stands up, he can see that there is a hole there. An absence. An empty space for him to fit himself into. To push and push what is not there, hard and hard, harder than ever before.

This is the moment Anders has been waiting for.

18.

The old man at the bar introduces himself and offers to buy me a drink. The next thing I know, we are sitting at a table with a pitcher between us and Francis is talking about the old days, which I assume means back when he still had hair. I am unable to look at Francis objectively at this point since I have imbibed way too much alcohol for that, but he seems harmless enough. I am focusing on loosening the tether until I feel totally free of it, so I am not listening to him as closely as I should.

This becomes clear to me when he leans across the table, which rocks unsteadily until it decides to slope in my direction. A puddle of beer trickles toward me, so I block the oncoming tide with one arm. The wetness soaks into the sleeve of my blouse.

My thinking is skewed too. I too am off balance. I want to tip over so far I fall into another way of being.

"You're a beautiful woman," Francis is saying, his words tumbling over each other in their rush to get away from him. "If I was younger I'd want nothing more than to take you home and screw you 'til the sun come up."

A man like all men. No different from the animals.

"But you remind me of my sister," Francis is saying. "And looking at you like that would make me cry." When he lifts his mug it is shaking and slopping beer. Somehow he manages to drink deeply. Now I am listening. "She passed a long time ago, when we were just kids."

I dole out the proper verbiage, sip my beer. It is sad when young people die but, after all, every story has the same unhappy ending.

Francis rubs the top of his smooth head with one grimy hand. His nails are the permanent black of a car mechanic. His faded leather jacket is worn through in places and too large for his bony frame. He has utilized a piece of rope in place of a belt. Francis reminds me of the residents I work with every day. Perhaps he is one of them.

"She was murdered. And the son of a bitch who killed my kid sister never got caught. He would have lived out his life free and clear, but I couldn't let that happen.

Wasn't right. Why should that motherfucker get to go on living? Why should he eat pizza and jerk off while my sister rotted away six feet under? No, I couldn't let it go. Wasn't in me to do that."

I can hear Ben laughing with a group of women behind me. He moves around the room, clearing glasses off tables and wiping down the wood with the damp dish rag. I look over Francis' head to check the clock above the bar. Thirty more minutes until Ben closes the place down. I sip my drink.

"So I fuckin' killed him myself," Francis says. "And I'll tell you this. I don't feel one iota of remorse. The fucker deserved it. My sister was beautiful, she was real smart, she was going places. He was a sick fuck, a predator. He stalked her and took her life. So fuck it: I took his."

Francis starts to cough. He is working himself up over this bit of history or fantasy, whatever this is he is telling me.

Whatever.

Ben comes to our table. "Are you all right, Franny?" he asks.

Franny? How odd. Another Franny, and wearing a black leather jacket. Not believing I will find anything, I lean over and examine the old guy's left shoulder.

Sure enough, the snake patch is there.

The room spins. The acrid smell of grilled meat is making me nauseous. I excuse myself to head for the rest room while Ben gets a glass of water for Francis.

Franny.

I walk to the bar, then down the length of it to the narrow hall that leads to the rest rooms. Van Morrison's "Comfortably Numb" is playing on the jukebox.

When I enter the tiny bathroom, I am thinking about the bartender. This other woman's life. What it would be like to be her, living out here in the world of the living. Instead of tucked away in the unreal world of other people's dreams that feel like life, and life that feels like nothing at all.

I no longer want the life I have. I never chose my work. My work chose me. Now I want to choose my own life. I want to choose who to be.

I pull up my skirt and squat above the unpleasant toilet seat. Ben should put a little more elbow grease into cleaning the rest rooms. I pee, then wash my hands in cold water. The hot tap is broken. The small oval mirror over the white porcelain sink is speckled with dried soap. In between the grey patches I can see my face and it is not a reassuring sight. My eyes are empty, my cheeks sunken, my skin like paste. I look like a dead woman, a cadaver ready for advanced biology class. I don't look like me.

I look like one of the residents, someone suffering from an incurable case of SIPD.

When I return to the barroom, I check myself out in the mirror behind the bar. I look like me again. I am sort of pale all over and fuzzy, like I have been drinking. But I no longer look like a dead body, like something out of a horror movie.

I stop to stare at myself for a minute, pretending to fuss with my hair. I do look like Virginia, but I am not her. This remains disappointing.

Francis and Ben are talking quietly at the table but both men shut up and gape at me when I sit down.

"What?" I ask, but neither man responds.

The smell of char-broiled beef hits me hard once again and I put my face in my hands. I remain still like this. I am trying not to vomit.

Ben whispers, "What happened to her?"

Francis is silent. I imagine he shrugs, or maybe he points to the empty pitcher on the table to indicate the blame for my condition resides with the alcohol they both encouraged me to consume. Or allowed me to consume. Who am I kidding? *I* chose to drink here tonight, my condition has nothing to do with them. My eyes remain closed.

I can hear them whispering but I am not listening. Blah blah blah. Talk all you want, I am thinking.

Then my thoughts darken until there is only the darkness inside my head, a blackness growing blacker. Like a starless, moonless night on the beach.

Gradually the bar buzz recedes. I can no longer smell that awful odor. I can no longer feel the presence of the two men on either side of me, the press of the back of my thighs against the chair I am sitting in, the weight of my head in my hands.

All of the sensory data around me has disappeared. Nothing is left, not even a thought.

I am the absence of thought.

19.

What Anders knows is this: when someone else is drunk enough or high enough or traumatized into a state of shock or in a coma or near death, that is the moment. That is when you can find a place for yourself, move in and slip inside. That is when you can press hard, hard and harder, until it happens. And you do it. You change. You change into someone else.

The woman is naked and the hole gapes like the hole in a bagel and it is asking to be filled with something made of flesh and meat and air, something that can be pushed inside hard and harder. The nothing that is there, it is there asking to be remade, to be made into something, something that feels.

When the gun goes off people are screaming and there is the deafening sound of solid material tearing or bursting. Thoughts formed from a new type of thought entirely enter Anders' mind in a gentle flow. He thinks: You dream you are the people you dislike. There is no escaping your dreams. Sometimes you cannot wake yourself up. None of us can do anything about who we are in the darkness of our own minds.

Anders lies on his back on the sticky floor that smells of rubber and smoke and flat beer. His eyes are closed but he sees it anyway and it is rising from his chest where a hole has formed, a big bloody hole. It rises above the tables and Anders wills it to go just a few feet more. He wills it with everything that is in him to go into the woman.

The double wail of an ambulance siren fills in the hole that is the distance, growing louder and closing up the gap until it is filling Anders' head with the promise of sorrow and pain. His chest is wailing too, blowing and raining like some tropical storm. He can no longer see what rose from his chest to hover above him, to float above the barroom, to flit like a cloud above the blonde head of the woman as she hugged herself, curled tight in the lap of her chair, weeping and shaking.

20.

Ben is driving me home in a car he has borrowed from someone. When I try to open my eyes, I realize they are already open. I feel like I am dreaming, but instead I am living.

Ben is talking about the number of young people who are suffering from mental illness these days. He is talking about the increasing speed of onset for the various personality fragmentation disorders in college-age students and kids in their twenties. He is saying it is a plague, a modern-day plague.

"The idea that these disorders can be fixed or controlled is a fantasy promoted by the public relations departments of the multinational pharmaceutical corporations. It's a joke. I mean, all I see are people going off the deep end. Like that guy tonight. I don't see anyone getting better. I don't see the students who have SIPD graduating with honors and getting good jobs, thanks to their daily doses of Adjuster. You know what I mean?"

I do know what Ben means.

"What happened with the lawn guy?" I ask.

I cannot seem to rein in my untethered mind. Flashes of memory spark on and off. Francis and the silver gun, the little baby gun he slipped from a pocket of his leather jacket. The smell of gasoline and big hands wrapped around my throat. Noise, blood, sirens, screams. The man who mows the lawn with the hole blowing open, the gaping hole. The skeleton in the mirror. A snake patch on the sleeve. The storm, the college photo, the number one hundred and eleven. The emptiness, and the alarm bell going off in my head, an alarm that is still ringing.

My memories are like a movie without continuity, a slide show out of order.

"What lawn guy?" Ben asks. "Are you all right? Jeezus. Vic is going to blame *me* when I show up with you in this condition. I mean, how many drinks did you have tonight?"

Vic? As in *Victor*? What does *he* have to do with tonight and Ben and me and my condition? The fire alarm bell in my head is banging itself on the sides of my skull. I roll down the window, and as I do so I realize we are near the beach. And we are riding in an old Volkswagen.

"What year is this?" I ask about the car. It looks like an antique.

Ben gives me a baleful glance. He sighs heavily. "Vic is not going to be happy about this," he mutters to himself, ignoring my question.

The full moon looks smaller in the wide dark sky, and softer, dimmer, as if it might be slowly receding into tomorrow. We are driving fast on the deserted ocean highway. I lean back against the headrest and close my eyes. The alarm in my mind keeps on ringing, but quieter now. I have a feeling of distance, as if everything I once knew has been left far behind.

I do not want to go back to work tomorrow. I do not want to go back to my office on the quad, Celia and her ugly dreams, Justin and his hallucinatory thefts, Sasha and her hot pink napkin arrangements, the nothingness of my bottles of Diet-Water, the loneliness inside everyone's head. Especially the loneliness inside my own head.

"Hey, Ben, can we stop for a while, maybe take a walk on the beach?"

He sighs and says, "When I called Vic I said I would have you home in half an hour. That was an hour and a half ago. He's gonna blame me for this and I don't want to have to try to tell him it was all your idea. Give me a break, Virginia. Okay?"

I am stunned into silence. Is he kidding? Why is he calling me by that name? And why does he keep talking about someone named Vic? What for? Is he playing some kind of sick game here?

My heart begins to pound and I grab onto the door handle with my right hand. Maybe I can jump out the next time he slows down. Like at a stop sign or a traffic light.

We continue to speed along through the salty blackness, our headlights following the curve of the double yellow lines running down the middle of the road. Eventually I let go of the door handle.

Ben slows the car to a crawl and we turn down a dirt drive.

The car sputters. It's got to be one of those battered VW Bugs owners keep on the road with chewing gum and super glue. My brother had a Volksie like that when I was in high school. I used to drive it to the beach late at night, sleepy and stoned, my high school boyfriend in the passenger seat. I drove barefoot. Sometimes all I wore were the marks from his hands.

"What would you do with you if you were me?" I ask and Ben smiles. Sure enough, his dimple is visible in the dark.

"I would give me the morning shift *and* the night shift tomorrow," he says, looking at me like this is funny. "I mean today, of course. It's going on four a.m., in case you're wondering."

I don't know what he means by shifts, but I hang my head out the window so I can watch the stars fade out.

Ben blames the drugs, the corporations, the technology. This seems much too convenient. I think it is my fault, actually. Maybe I am the dreamer. Or maybe I *was* the dreamer.

I can no longer hear the alarm bell in my head. Maybe the past is really over, and this is something else. Maybe there is only one real moment and it is now. Maybe we are driving into the future I dreamed about or created for myself from the absence, from the most important nothingness. Maybe I've changed, or changed places.

Or maybe I've just fucked up.

When Ben stops the car and cuts the engine, we are in front of my office building. We sit quietly as the cheap gas in the engine knocks around for a minute. The foxtail palms swish their fronds, making a sound like a Hawaiian grass skirt. The quad is empty and artificially bright from all the mandatory street lamps. My office window is dark, but Victor's is not.

"If you ever need a quick score, come check out the numbers on my office door," I tell Ben. He looks at me strangely and says nothing.

"Not tonight, Virginia," he says quietly. "I like my job and I want to keep it. I mean, I feel weird enough being out so late together." He frowns and opens his door. "Guess I'll walk back. I doubt I can get a cab at this hour."

I climb out my side. "Why don't you take the car?" I ask, puzzled.

"You mean it?" Ben says, then slams his door and restarts the engine. "I'll have it back at the bar by noon. Don't worry, I'll drive slow. I'll coast home. Really, I will," Ben promises, his voice earnest and eager. His teeth shine in the street light. "Thanks, Virginia," he says as he pulls away from the curb.

I'm shaking my head. So weird. Ben acted like I was lending him the car. Or *Virginia* was lending him the car, but he was thanking *me*.

My mind begins to swell up like a wet napkin. I stand under the street light and watch the non-native geckos run up and down the cement pole, gobbling up our native bugs.

I do not feel like going inside. I am not sure why Ben dropped me off here. How does he know where my office is located? I do not remember telling him this, but in my inebriated state I might have told him anything. Maybe I told him my name is really Virginia and I live here with a guy named Vic. Why I would do such a thing, I am unable to fathom.

I look up at Victor's window again. Unlike my office, Victor's suite has a bed. And two couches, two comfortable powder blue couches. And since the light is on, maybe I will not disturb him too much if I knock on his door. Maybe he will take pity on me and let me stretch out on one of his soft sofas.

Victor to the rescue again.

The god upstairs.

I walk up the front steps and let myself into the lobby. I pull the dead bolt into place. There are no lights on so I use my feet to feel my way across the wrinkled linoleum to the bottom of the staircase. Then I continue up the two flights to Victor's floor.

The hallway is dimly lit by a row of wall sconces, so I find the apartment easily and knock lightly on the door. I am totally exhausted and can hardly keep my eyes open. What a night. All the walking, the alcohol, then the violence. My body isn't used to this. I lean against the wall and shut my eyes for a moment, waiting for the door to open.

The darkness is thick inside my head, thick and soupy. The me inside my mind also closes my eyes. A moment passes.

When I try to open my eyes I realize they are already open. Victor stands in the doorway in a faded pair of jeans and a sleeveless undershirt. He reaches for me just as I fall into his arms. But when he pulls me to his chest and sweeps me into the apartment, I can feel the tension in his body. It is like something coiled, tight and hard.

"That's it," he says sharply and lets go of me so suddenly I slip to the floor. He's replaced the ugly green carpet with laminated wood. How did he do that so quickly?

"I like your floor," I tell him and he growls like an angry animal.

Are we any different at all? I think not.

I am glancing around at his apartment and it is nothing like I remember. A huge dining table made from black stone dominates the room, and beyond that a love seat and overstuffed chairs in white linen. The art on the wall is abstract and flashy. The lights are recessed around a rattan fan in a high white ceiling. A life-size blown glass statue of mating iguanas in clashing shades of orange and green poses confidently by the front window.

Victor yanks me to my feet just so he can shove me against the wall. Then he rubs his hands up and down my body with a little too much force, but not enough to hurt me. "It's extremely late," he says in a gruff voice, "and I couldn't sleep because I was thinking about you."

Like you are thinking about me now? I want to ask him. Because he is hard against my thigh, so hard I am not sure this is such a bad thing for us. Us, together in this moment.

I lick his fleshy lips and he suckles my tongue. His mouth tastes of mint and lemon, of a recent toothbrushing. When I touch his face with my hand he slaps it away. His eyes are black saucers, empty bagel holes. He is angry but he wants to fuck me too much to talk about it right now.

He pins my arms over my head and I close my eyes and the alarm bell is silent and the blackness is nice and familiar and he smells like beer unless that is me and he presses his body against me, covering me with his hot heavy flesh, until I start to feel like I can no longer breathe and then I cough and cough and the fragmented memories, the nightmarish images start coming at me again.

I remember the beach, the smell of salt and iodine, the cool wind from the east and the hard-packed sand. But the beach does not remember me. The blowing sand, the frothing waves, the incoming tide erase the memory of me, erase all traces of the moment and of themselves in that moment. Over and over, replacing themselves in the moment with the beautiful industry of nature's recycling.

I remember how I lay on my back on the beach and the stars were pinpricks in a black velour backdrop. The waves pulled and sucked at my cold skin, lapping and slapping my unmoving legs and feet.

I am not certain how long I played my high school boyfriend's games, and I am not so sure they were all his. But I played Joey's games. I let it happen and continue to happen. Over and over again.

Then we stopped. Just like that. We both left town, we went our separate ways to our separate colleges. Joey never called or wrote to me, and I thought I felt good about that.

When I came home for the weekend in the autumn of my junior year, I was taking a break from everything. My latest boyfriend and I had been fighting a lot and I felt confused. My parents were stupidly pleased and my brothers all approved of the new guy, a psychology major who worked at McGoren's a few nights a week. We had only slept together once, however, and the sex was a complete failure. He wanted another try and was pushing to go away together for a weekend, but I was stalling. The thought of two days and nights in bed with a mentally stable, good-looking, decent sort of guy who did nothing to turn me on was depressing. So I cut out for home instead.

Kip managed the Dome Gym on Second Street, and Thom worked at a New York style restaurant a few blocks away. Franny had dropped out of grad school and was hanging around in his beat-up leather jacket, pontificating and looking iffy.

I walked the beach and drove around town in Thom's ancient VW Bug. I drank beers and smoked reefer at Kip's gym with my brothers and their townie friends. Kip let us bounce a basketball around the deserted gym once he'd closed up the building for the night. All the guys were big, they were all really built and they spent too much time looking at themselves in the wall-to-wall mirrors.

Time passed quickly on that visit. Time was passing like that suddenly, and it seemed to be passing faster and faster. Franny explained it like this: "You're growing up, kid. The older you get, the more anxious you get about your time. Because it's no longer infinite. And you don't want to waste what's left."

I did not think that was the source of my concern. I thought I had so much time left I was sure to waste most of it.

On my last night at home, I was in bed by eleven. I planned to get a good night's sleep, some sober and straight sleep, so my mind would be clear for the return trip to college. Thom was lending me his car so I would not have to go Greyhound back to school. I planned to get up at four and head out. But I lay awake for hours, the full moon sliding its bright yellow light across the floor and walls of my bedroom.

I felt stuck in my childhood, moored in my teenage angst. *I should never have come back here*, I was thinking. *I should have stayed away and become someone else.*

The cicadas were raucous. Occasionally, a deranged mockingbird called piteously for a mate. On the night stand next to my bed, I had one of those square digit clocks that click every time the numbers change. Click, click, twelve o'clock. Click, click, one o'clock. Click, one-eleven.

One-eleven. When I looked at the clock I saw a string of tall, thin, look-alike ones. Something inside my head burst free.

I knew in that moment. I knew what I wanted. I wanted to be someone else entirely. Someone who could feel more with less. Someone who had faith in her own inner meaning despite the absence of evidence to support that faith. Someone who followed her passions, someone who loved her life.

I wanted to be alive. Alive in the moment, in all moments. Alive with feelings and desire.

Then I heard someone moving around outside.

21.

Anders is bleeding from his chest. There is a hole there that goes right through his blue uniform shirt pocket that says *Joseph Anders, Lawn Maintenance.* A hole that is black and not empty but full, full of blood, bright red blood that keeps coming and coming.

Blood drips while he pushes and pushes against the front door with his shoulder and all his strength. He pushes hard and hard, harder. He is forcing the door to open. There is no other choice.

Anders saw her through the window. Not the usual window but the window up above that one. Her light is not on, but the lights are bright in the window above hers. The big guy who touched her in the rain, he's up there too.

Anders pushes and pushes. He groans with pain and strain until the door caves in with an explosive splintering sound.

He is not supposed to enter this building. Anders knows he does not have permission to go inside. He could get in trouble. He could get fired for this.

Anders steps into the dark lobby and looks around. His eyes see easily in the nighttime darkness. He is like an animal. Anders thinks he is no different than an animal and he is glad this is true.

He pulls himself up the stairs one at a time. The blood drips onto the steps as he moves up one stair and then rests, moves up one and rests. In his head, Anders hears the blood rushing slower and slower, like the sound of low tide as it recedes farther from shore.

He's dragging the left side of his body behind him like a duffel bag full of weights.

Anders shakes his head a little as he pulls himself along. He is dizzy and confused. He does not remember how he got to his usual spot on the bench in the quad across from the woman's building. He remembers looking into the loud smoky bar and he remembers going into the noise and the smoke, and he remembers walking up to the woman where she sat with her back to him at a round wooden table. He remembers how there was more noise and more smoke, but after that the night is a blank reel of film. Until he found himself here, outside her building, sitting on the bench. With a hole in his uniform and blood coming out. Lots of blood that is still coming out of the hole.

Time is not to be trusted. Anders know this, but he also knows there is not much of it left.

He crawls across the second floor landing to where he can see white light leaking out from under one of the doors. When he reaches his hand into the light, it is red with blood. His chest is wet against the floor beneath him. Bursting stars appear in front of him wherever he looks.

Anders tries to stand up but he is teetering. He tries to stay on his feet but he is falling forward. He tries to lean against the door to rest again, just for a moment, but the door opens, it was not locked, it was not even closed properly, and Anders tumbles forward into the apartment.

Just as he crashes onto the floor, he sees the woman. She is lying on her back only a few feet away. She is lying there on the wet sand. Her body is naked and blue.

The tide has gone all the way out and the night sky is full of stars. Mist settles over the beach like a sheet across an empty bed or a shroud on a frozen corpse. Anders thinks about how we are all made of crazy little molecules, dreams and dust, like the stars and the sand, the earth and the sea, the animals that we are.

He reaches for her. He reaches out and touches what he can change. He touches the changing woman so that he, too, can change.

Anders closes his eyes and allows the dream to continue.

22.

That night in my parents' house, in my childhood bedroom, I lay still and listened. I listened to the scratch of palm fronds rubbing themselves against my bedroom window. Then I heard it again.

There is no escaping your dreams. Especially when they come for you in the night.

I rolled out of bed and tiptoed from my room, down the unlit hall past the master suite where my parents lay sleeping. Downstairs, I stood in front of the sliding glass doors. Cool air seeped through the narrow spaces around the perimeter of the sliders. I was unable to see into the back yard, but I left the light on and unlocked one of the doors with a loud click.

There are just so many wrong turns you can take. And all of them end up in the same place. In that final moment. The last moment of the dream of your life.

I step out into the dim orange glow around the entryway, my hands folded now as if in prayer. Sliding the door closed behind me, I walk ahead into the blinding blackness of the back yard. The wind is stronger and meaner than I expected. The tall ficus hedge around the boundary of the yard bends and bows, while the palm trees whip their heads like go-go dancers.

The ground is damp under my bare feet as I walk away from the light and into the cold dark center of the night. The yard has been freshly mowed and the blades of grass stick to my soles. It smells like fresh cut grass and something else. Grilled meat.

An arm hooks around my neck from behind, then a rough hand closes over my mouth and I bite down hard enough to taste blood. His hand is salty but the skin reeks of gasoline, so I begin to cough. He keeps the hand over my mouth and I keep coughing until I start to feel like I am suffocating. I struggle until he lets go of my mouth to pin both of my arms against my sides.

Like seeks like, after all.

It has been three years and he has grown taller and stronger, his body more wiry and tough. His face is twisted, angry and hard. I suddenly know that he is a different person than the boy I fooled around with so many times. This young man is emptier and more violent. He is less and more at the same time.

"You little shit," is how my high school boyfriend greets me. "You fucking scag."

His grip on my arms tightens as I realize just how much I am not enjoying this. It no longer feels like a game I am willing to play. Before I can say anything, he punches me in the face and the pain explodes inside my head. Then nothing. I feel nothing.

When I come to, my nose is dripping blood on my chest and I am slumped in the passenger seat of a car speeding through the night. My feet are ankle deep in fast food wrappers and sticky Styrofoam cups. I'm naked except for a blue uniform jacket draped across my chest. The blood from my nose soaks through it onto my breasts. "Comfortably Numb" is on the radio.

A pair of pantyhose is wrapped tight around my neck. The nylons are tied too tight, the bulky knot pressing against the base of my throat.

"You think I don't know what you been doing?" he says before he slaps me on the ear. I lean away, leaning as far as I can until my head is resting against the car door. "I heard. I went up there and saw you with my own eyes. I know what you been doing."

Rain drizzles across the windshield but Joey does not turn on his wipers. He turns off the headlights and steers the car into an empty parking lot. I recognize the beach rest rooms under the dull glow of a street lamp. He drives toward the beach and parks facing the ocean, far enough from the street lights so we are sitting in the dark. Then he yanks his jacket off my body and tosses it into the back seat. I am naked and cold.

He pulls my head around by jerking on the pantyhose. His mouth is as hot and hard as his flesh, like a sun-soaked stone. He pushes into me hard, hard and harder, like he wants to push through me to the far side of the world.

I feel nothing at first, then I feel everything at once.

He reaches across me to open my door and shoves me out onto the asphalt. I am up on my knees crawling across the gravel and sand when he climbs out after me. He laughs a little and kicks me lightly in the ribs, lifting me with the toe of his boot. The same way you would turn over a dead animal after you ran it over with your car. I spill onto my back and stare up at him. Around his head the stars form a crown of light.

"Get up, Virginia," he says in a low voice, then he crouches over me and lightly strokes my stomach with one index finger until I quiver.

It always ends up like this with me and men.

My hair is in my mouth and blood from my nose is collecting in my throat. The pantyhose around my neck makes me feel like I am choking. I sputter and turn my head to spit. He runs his hands over my hips and down between my thighs with just enough force to feel both good and bad at the same time.

When he stands up and pulls me to my feet I let him. When he sweeps me up in his arms and carries me across the dunes I let him. But when I turn my face into his chest I inhale gasoline fumes and I start to cough again.

He drops me in the sand and I lie back into the rhythm of the waves. The tide is out but we are near enough to the tide line to catch some spray. I can feel the waves pounding toward us, crashing onto the shore. Then I feel the pull as the waves drag themselves away from us again.

When Joey stretches out on the crusty sand beside me, I say, "Why do you smell like gasoline?"

"Occupational hazard," he explains. "I got a job at the garage on Eighth Street fixing cars. You know how good I am with my hands." My nose has stopped bleeding but there is a fat clot stuck in the back of my throat and whenever it tickles me, I start coughing. "The Mustang I'm driving tonight is one I'm working on now. Some rich dude owns it, runs a couple businesses downtown. Nice car. Classic lines and shit."

Is he looking for my approval? I give him nothing and he keeps talking. Maybe if I listen quietly he will go easy on me.

I give good ear. I give the best ear I have ever given.

"My job's good. I make okay money, I fuck around on my nights off, all's swell. I live okay without you and all our old shit, time passes and shit, you know. But your brother is a fucking pain up my ass, Virginia. Franny's a bum, face it. He comes into the garage and yaks, he has so much nothing to do. My sister this, my sister that. He wants me to hear, see? He wants me to know you don't give a shit about me anymore."

I stare straight up into the drizzling sky until the rain stings my eyes and I am forced to roll onto my side. I am freezing, but I will my teeth not to chatter so Joey will keep talking and not start on me.

"The fucking guy got me curious. Was it true what Franny was saying? That Virginia's now this pretty little coed with a dorm room full of books? The Virginia I knew was always crawling around on all fours, just waiting for me to let her out of her fucking cage."

The rain has stopped for a moment to catch its breath, but the waves keep on coming in and out in their endless pulsating rhythm. He pushes my shoulders back down onto the sand and rolls on top of me. His chest has filled out and the curly hairs tickle my sore nose. He slides down until his head is between my breasts.

"I had to go and check things out for myself." His voice is muffled. "I tracked old Virginia through campus housing. Simple enough. Then I sat on a bench in the quad and ate a cheeseburger, waiting for her to come out of her dorm. I waited and waited like some fucking loyal dog. And suddenly, there she was. It was Virginia all right, but she had a whole new look. All prim and proper in her long straight skirt and stiff white blouse, her fucking nylon stockings and flat shoes. Looked like somebody else, some uptight bitch I didn't know."

He shifts his weight on me. His voice is a low growl. "I followed her around campus all afternoon, from building to building, waiting outside in the fucking sun and the fucking rain and the goddam boring dark. I followed her off campus too. All the way to the hot shit college scene downtown. Big fucking deal, right? Suddenly she ducked into some dive bar. So I stood outside that dumpy shithole and watched her run around behind the bar. I waited there while she let all the guys paw her for tips. For shitty tips! I stood out there for hours and I got more and more pissed. You know why?"

He pauses, but I say nothing. I am nothing, I am nothing but a vessel into which he pours his sadness, his anger, his own nothingness.

"Because it was true what that fuck Franny had been saying. *This* Virginia did not give a shit about me. *My* Virginia, the Virginia I knew and loved, was gone! She'd changed so fucking much she was someone else. She was like a different person. Looking at this woman, you'd never believe she'd ever have anything to do with *me*. You'd never believe the things *I* could make her do. The things *she wanted me to do to her*."

I can feel the beat of the tide coming closer to us, the sound of the surf a furious pounding inside my head, a ringing, an internal alarm. I try not to breathe too deeply, I do not want to start coughing and choking again.

The wind splatters us with the ocean's salty spray.

"But I knew it was the same girl. The same Virginia," he whispers. "People can't change, not really. They can't change themselves *inside*."

He pushes and pushes hard, hard and harder, until he is so deep inside me we are the same person looking out his eyes. I am staring into my own sad green eyes and all I can see is the tiny reflection of Joey, and inside that is a tiny reflection of me. I am nothing in his eyes and he is less than nothing in mine.

"So here we are, lying on the beach. Together. Like no time has passed. Like nothing has changed." Joey laughs and says, "Everything starts and ends with me inside you, Virginia."

He pulls himself up, sliding himself over my chilled flesh, smearing himself on me like melted cheese on fries, until we lie face to face. His breath is hard and scratchy against my tender nose. When he wipes one hand across my swollen lips, it comes away covered in blood.

He is done with his story and I have listened to every word.

"Whatever you say, guy," I mutter. "*Whatever*," I say, and I mean it.

He pushes and pushes, hard and harder, until I begin to cough. I care but I do not care about what he is doing to my body. My body is not me, after all. He thinks he knows who he has been fucking and hurting and loving in some warped version of a human emotion, but he does not. The woman he has slapped and sucked and stalked and aroused and abused in so many ways, the woman underneath him, she just looks like me. She is not me. Not at all.

My indifference is total in this moment.

My acceptance of this moment is total.

It is raining hard now and the wind is howling and I am coughing when he puts his big hands around my throat and squeezes. The knot in the pantyhose, the clotted blood, the smell of gasoline and burgers and the night surf, the rain and wind. Everything becomes a weapon in certain situations.

I open my eyes wide until they bulge and I stare like this until the stars over his head, the crown of stars he wears like some ancient sea god, the pinpoints of light in the black shroud of night, zoom away. All the stars zoom away to the vanishing point.

And then they all blink out.

* * * *

All that is left is my throat and the need to let the night air inside and I am coughing and coughing. Something is blocking my windpipe, a cold lump lodged too tightly, and he is pressing against it with the pads of his meaty thumbs and I am gasping and flailing and trying to cough it out.

The thing in my throat.

"When your dreams are more real than your reality?"

It is Victor who is talking to me now. He is speaking in a faraway whisper. Victor the man has taken the place of Joey the boy, my high school boyfriend, the first person who taught me how to care and not care about myself. How to be someone else, yet more myself. Much more. It is Victor who is speaking to me from some distant time, another moment. But it is Joey who has his hands around my throat and he will not let go. He will never let go.

I look up and the sky is a mirror that is black with the night below. I look up and the sea and the stars and the blackness move in to surround me. I am no longer coughing but there is something still lodged in my throat, something cold and hard.

I open my eyes wider and I am pinned against the wall of Victor's living room and his thick body presses against me and his hands are around my neck and his iron clasp is forcing the thing in my throat to edge up my windpipe or my esophagus, whatever.

I am choking and, at the same time, the blockage in my throat is coming loose.

The air in the room is ice cold and the black sky in my mind folds in on itself and becomes even blacker. Victor is saying in that faraway voice, "When your dreams are this real, so much more real than your reality? Then how do you know? How do you know *which one is your real consciousness?*"

The snake patch on a leather jacket.

The number one hundred and eleven.

A mirror with someone else's reflection.

A certain kind of personality. Smart, not slick.

When you really don't care about anything.

Interchangeable living beings. No different from the animals.

SIPD, that is, when we are no longer who we think we are.

I cough harder than I have ever coughed before and the thing, whatever it is, slides up past the back of my tongue. I close my eyes and gag. The thing feels huge in my mouth, round and smooth as a bullet, metallic tasting. The coughing stops and I try to spit it out.

"The self you believe is yourself is not the real you," Victor is saying. He lets go of my neck and my head sags forward until my chin rests on my chest. "If we can destroy the false self, that will be our salvation. Yours and mine."

I slide down the wall until I am sprawled across his polished wood floor. Victor kneels down by my head. When he reaches his finger into my mouth and clears out the air passage, I realize he has done this before.

The object drops from my slack mouth and falls to my chest, tumbling forward and coming to rest on the cliff of my left breast. The object settles there on the edge of a black hole that has opened in the thin skin right above my heart.

The hole is open and empty and full of blood and full of whatever it is inside me that remains intact. In spite of everything, in spite of the pain of remembering and the agony of forgetting, in spite of whatever comes up in the moments that make us who we are. The moments that make us alive.

When I look down at the object on the hole in my chest, it is with eyes that are bulging and blind. But I can see that the object is not a bullet but a key.

A key. A tiny metal key.

The key to a cage or a prison cell or an office or a bar or a private room in a hotel for sick people, a luxury apartment in the best part of town. The key to a secret or a life or a love or a personality. The key to freedom. The key to everything and to nothing at all.

Victor grabs me under the armpits and attempts to lift me into a sitting position, but my body is dead weight. When he lets go of me, I can feel myself falling. I fall a long, long way until at last I sink down into the floor like a six-foot hole in the hard-packed sand.

He cups my left breast in his hand and whispers, "Virginia."

I open myself to him and the waves and the night and the wind and the animals inside us.

23.

I try to open my eyes until I realize they are already open. Victor lies beside me, his big hand on my still quivering thigh. The recessed lighting hurts so I shade my eyes as I look around at the apartment. It is bigger than I remember and well appointed. The man has money and taste.

Apartments, names, personalities, memories and everything else? Maybe all of it, all of us, are as interchangeable as the clouds in the sky.

"What happened to the lawn guy?" I ask, ruining Victor's moment.

"You don't remember?" he says in a bland monotone. "Why doesn't this surprise me?" He rolls onto his side and moves his hand up the inside of my thigh in one grand sweeping motion. I shudder. "Let's take a bath," he says.

He stands and reaches for my hands to pull me up. His face is in shadow and as far away as tonight's moon.

He is annoyed when I fail to remember things. Sometimes he gets angry and we fight, then have angry sex. Sometimes he sulks and withdraws. But I hate to remember. The past is over and has nothing to do with who I am now. And who I am now is all that interests me at the moment. That was then and this is now, I am thinking. This is me, living in the now.

He walks me through a vast bedroom toward the master bath. The unmade bed is king size, silky sheets in a rumpled pile. A rattan fan circulates the air around scattered piles of magazines and books. A flat screen television takes up most of one white wall. There is a mirror on the ceiling and when I look up I can see who I am.

I am Virginia, the woman behind the bar.

I have a name now.

I sit on the toilet while Victor (Vic?) runs the tap to fill the roman tub with hot water. He lights a dozen stubby candles that lean in crazy directions on the ledges around the tub, then flicks off the fluorescent light overhead. His shadow stretches and bounces around the room as he pulls his undershirt over his head and slides out of his jeans.

The sound of rushing water fills my head. Warm steam swirls into my eyes and nose and ears. The candles ooze their gentle scents, vanilla and almond. Victor squats in front of me and rests his arms on my knees, waiting for the tub to fill.

I am about to ruin this moment too when Victor covers my mouth with his hand and says, "Shut up, now. Not one fucking word, Virginia."

He gets in the tub. I step out of my clothes and, when Victor signals me with his index finger, I step in. While he softly soaps my shoulders and breasts, my arms and wrists and hands, Victor talks and I listen.

I guess Virginia is a good listener. She is all ears.

"You look around like this is a whole new world to you. It all seems new, doesn't it? All fresh and new." He laughs, his head thrown back. "Honey, you may not know where you are tonight, but let me tell you something. It doesn't matter. Not really. Because the truth is, you're in the same place everybody else is. It's just a moment in time. We're all in this moment together. Together. And that's all any of us have."

He scoops up my hair and cradles my head in one wide palm, then he pours on the shampoo. When he massages my scalp I let out a little moan and he laughs again.

"The present moment only lasts a few seconds," he says. "The moment is like a dream. It may feel like it continues for minutes or hours or days, but really, it only lasts a few seconds. And then we move on to the next moment. We live like this, we live from moment to moment, and all these moments are piling up inside our minds, forming our memories, forming a continuity, a coherent story of who we think we are."

"Victor," I say, "please tell me what happened to the lawn guy."

He stops rinsing my hair and sighs. The bathtub faucet is drip, drip, dripping. It sounds like my office clock ticking over and over, faster and faster.

Victor says, "One more time, woman. One more time. Every day you push me away, every night you fuck me like an animal. Every morning you do not remember, every night I must tell you again how it is here, what is real and what is not real, the story you are unable to tell yourself without me." He pauses, his voice tender. "One more time, I will fill in the holes, all those empty spaces you seem unable to fill in yourself."

His voice drifts by my ears, fainter now and wet, steamy. "There is no lawn guy. No Anders, no Joey, no Joe. No Celia, no Justin, no Sasha or Ben. No SIPD, no Malaise Group, no Diet-Water, no Francis in a barroom, no shots fired, no holes in anyone's chest. Do you understand me, Virginia?"

I open my eyes a crack and I am alone in the bathroom. Alone, alone, alone. Victor is gone, but his voice continues, a whisper now inside my head. "There is no Victor, no Vic, no god upstairs. I am part of the dream, the dream you need to wake up from. You need to wake up now so that you and I, together, can live wholly in this world. Do you understand, Virginia?"

And then my eyes are wide open and I am sputtering and choking. I am swallowing water and coughing it back up and swallowing more. Victor or Anders or Joey, a man has his hands around my neck and he is squeezing the base of my throat and I am suffocating and drowning and my feet are blue and my eyes are bulging and the sound of the sea beats against my brain and I close my eyes and I let it all go.

I let the moment go.

ABOUT THE AUTHOR

Originally from Boston, Mickey J. Corrigan lives and writes in the lush ruins of South Florida. Recent books include the edgy novellas in The Hard Stuff series (*Whiskey Sour Noir*, *Vodka Warrior*, *Tequila Dirty*, and *RealLife Rum*); the thrillers *Sugar Babies* and *The Ghostwriters*; and the spoofy crime novels *The Blow Off* and *Ex-Treme Measures*. Salt Publishing will release her new novel, *Project XX*, in 2017.